Revelations

By

Donald Morrison

Dark Forest Publishing

ISBN-13: 978-0692818824

ISBN-10: 0692818820

BISAC: Fiction / Psychological

First Edition

http://www.MorrisonStories.com

Printed in the United States of America

"We think sometimes that poverty is only being hungry, naked and homeless. The poverty of being unwanted, unloved, and uncared for is the greatest poverty of all."

-Mother Teresa-

This book is dedicated to the homeless population. Some of us believe there is still hope..

Revelations

The sun was bright in the sky, blasting its summer rays down on the dirty Los Angeles streets. It was a usual August day, mid-nineties and dry, the type of heat that made your skin feel like the layer of sunburn was being airbrushed on by the searing breeze.

Terrance Williams was under the awning of his local café in Silver Lake, sipping his ice water from the small plastic cup the barista inside had been kind enough to give him. He was grateful for the cool liquid, and shade bearing cloth above his head. When you're homeless, you come to find out that it truly is the little things that matter.

Terrance sat there for a moment, relishing the icy sensation as the cool liquid washed away the dry parchment that had coated the inside of his throat. He realized that he had begun to sweat, and when he looked down, the ice that had been floating listlessly in his cup had melted, and that the condensation that had been coating the cup had disappeared.

He leaned forward and felt his shirt slowly pull itself away from the chair before contacting wetly against the skin of his back. He took a deep breath and realized that the air had become extremely dry, and that it was like breathing the steam that wafted from the top of the free soup he received from the grimy kitchen he visited in downtown from time to time.

He looked up, bringing his arm up to shield the increasingly bright sky from his vision when a flash caught his eyes. Across the street, the top of one of the towering palm trees that reached upwards ignited into a ball of fire, making it look like an oversized candle sticking oddly out of the concrete.

Immediately following the ones standing to its sides began to repeat the process. Almost instantly the street was transformed into a long, concrete birthday cake, complete with sparklers as transformers blew, sending showers of molten fragments outwards behind puffs of acrid smoke.

Terrance felt the skin on his arm beginning to become unbearably hot, and as he lowered it he saw a girl in high-waisted shorts and a loose fitting top running down the street screaming. Her skin was bright pink; quickly turning crimson, and he could see where her clothing was beginning to smoke. She had made it about twenty feet when her hair ignited and she lost her footing, crashing hard to the pavement and began writhing for a moment before her flesh ignited like everything else around her.

Terrance began to feel fear beyond anything he could recall. He watched the world around him burst into flames, and as he looked down at his own hands, saw the skin becoming transparent and blistering outwards.

Wednesday the 19th

Terrance shot awake, his heart pounding loudly against his ribs, his eyes moist from tears that had been falling backwards down his cheeks to his pillow. He could still feel his skin burning beneath the thin t-shirt he wore to keep warm on the summer nights. He sat up shaking, and held his hands in front of his face in the dim light, afraid that he'd see the blistered pockmarks where his skin should have been.

"T-Bone. T-Bone, you alright in there?"

The words were coming from the tarp covered *house* next to his. It was his newest acquaintance, Guitar Joe calling out.

After a moment he saw that the Guinness hued skin across the back of his hands were unscathed, and realized he was fine. It had just been a very vivid dream; a nightmare.

"Yeah Joe," he called out, his voice cracking through the air of his tent. "I'm ok... Just a bad dream, that's all."

4

"All right. Well, I gots me some mo vodka if'n you need it. Help ya sleep better."

His friend was never short of two things; willingness to share everything he had with those around him, and vodka.

"Thanks Joe," he called back, the vision still persisting in front of him. "I'm good man.   Maybe take you up on that tomorrow though, it's gonna be my birthday."

"Well happy birthday T-Bone." Joe called back.

Terrance started to call out that it was the next day, but realized the lack of point it would of made, and simply said, "Thanks Joe," before laying back down and letting his eyes focus on the picture of what had been his wife and boy in front of the house he'd been thrown out of fifteen years prior.

He settled back in, not bothering to pull the worn out sleeping bag back up to cover himself. He was still soaked in sweat, and his heart was beating rapidly, the flowing blood keeping him warm enough that the cool air on his skin felt good.

He lay there for quite some time, listening to his pulse beating rhythmically in his ears, the image of the young girl catching fire scorched into his vision.

He tried thinking about a time in his life that he'd had a dream so vivid, but every thought was pulled back to that girl, and the feeling of his flesh beginning to boil from the heat.

He lay there for another few moments, and then decided to take a stroll; an attempt to clear the thoughts that were now festering out of his head.

He kicked the bag off and sat up, reaching out to grab his beyond worn leather boots at the foot of his house. He pulled them on and tied the laces tight before grabbing one of his three t-shirts and pulling it over his head.

"Travel light," he'd always said.

He unzipped the front and slowly stepped out onto his *porch*; the sidewalk that ran under the overpass on Alvarado, where the 101 freeway ran overhead.

He moved from place to place, but for the last year and a half, this little stretch of concrete had been his home, shared along side a handful of others that had found themselves "down on their luck" as they referred to it.

He stepped into the cool night air, the sounds of traffic overhead filling his ears, and the sound of a helicopter in the distance reminding him that he was still in the big city, and not North Carolina where he'd lived for over four decades.

He decided to take a stroll up to the park that was a short walk away. He liked strolling around the lake in Echo Park. The sound of the fountain, and ducks playing in the water was the most soothing reminder of nature that he could afford to enjoy. Since he had lost his job, his house, and his family; it was the little things he had come to rely upon to keep in touch with his humanity. He couldn't afford to take a vacation, and when you only made around thirty dollars a day, if you were lucky, taking a trip was a luxury that could not be afforded. He'd learned his lesson once before about leaving his house unattended when he took a trip to San Diego, and came back two days later to everything he owned being gone; cleared out by city workers. He had lost everything he had that wasn't in the backpack he had taken with him; his passport, his family photos, everything that he had cherished, gone, thrown away by a person that didn't know, or care about the importance of his belongings. Now he stayed close to his house, except for when he was out working, which for him, was asking for change at the Alvarado and Glendale intersection. It was what he and his friends referred to as "good reality", and a space that had gotten him in more than one territory fights.

He made his way up the street, enjoying the fact that when it was early dusk, the city wasn't screaming with the sounds of traffic and piercing sirens.

The brisk air felt good against his skin and he realized that his shirt was beginning to dry. In twenty minutes he was walking around the edge of the lake, the smell of water and moss filling his senses. He strolled slowly around the reservoir, taking everything in, feeling grateful that it was still extremely early, and none of the new neighborhood people were out and about yet.

Echo Park had changed drastically over the last ten years. What was once a neighborhood where all manner of folks could hang out, and mingle, lazing about around the lake, drinking their beer, or playing cards at the tables, now was filled with close minded, middle class transplants, that had moved in, and through a process that the rich folk were referring to as *gentrification*, had pushed all the old neighborhood natives out, and replaced them with a younger, hip culture of rude, insensitive, twenty-something's that acted a manner of which screamed insecurity and lack of respect.

Terrance reminisced as he made his laps around the lake of times when he'd see other homeless people, or the old neighborhood gangsters listening to oldies music, and families with children all occupying the same space, sharing the same barbeque areas, and play areas with their kids. Now however, if you were homeless, or didn't fit into a societal stereotype, the police would show up, run your name and take you in if you had any warrants, or tell you to get out of the park. It seemed as if humanity in general had formed a loathing for anyone who didn't fit into their perfect design; homeless, gutterpunks, the mentally ill that had been thrown out on the streets by Reagan in the eighties.

Right now however, in the pre-dawn veil of darkness, he was at peace, unbothered by the slumbering world of fear and insecurity around him. At the very moment, it was just him and the ducks.

He walked around the lake once more, his mind finally pulling itself away from the graphic dream, easing slowly back into a state of calm.

As he made his way down Sunset the sky began to take on the azure hue that prefaced the sunrise. He decided to make his way to the local café instead of heading back to his house; if he was lucky, Armando would be opening shop, and would make sure that he "dropped" one of the muffins in the delivery.

He strolled to the café, enjoying the morning glow that accompanied the city coming to life, the thrum of traffic, busses going by with tired faces lining the windows, the smell of the local bakeries cooking their morning supplies.

When he arrived at the Tropical, Armando was putting the patio furniture out.

"Hey T-Bone." Armando said with a friendly smile and a single nod of the head that old Los Angeles still lingered in.

"Morning to you as well." Terrance replied equally curt. "What you got brewin' this morning?"

Armando finished pushing the last chair in and turned to Terrance with a smile. "We got that Ethiopian you like back in."

"That's the one that tastes like blueberries right?" Terrance asked, a smile growing across his face.

"That's the one."

"Well I got about two bucks on me, that gonna be able to cover it?" Terrance asked.

He knew it wasn't, he'd looked at the menu enough times to know the coffee started at three fifty and worked its way up; he was just ashamed to ask for a discount because of his situation. He'd been on the streets for years, but there were just some things he couldn't kick, and being ashamed of having to beg was one of those things.

Armando smiled, and nodded towards the entrance before tapping Terrance's arm and stepping inside. "Yeah, I was thinking about making a special today, coffee and a muffin for two bucks," he paused shooting a grin at Terrance, "but you better hurry, because I can't run this special all day."

"Thanks Armando," Terrance said as he stepped over the threshold into the silent café.

"No problem T-Bone, I know how things can get. I just hope that if I ever end up in a tough spot, people would be willing to help me like I have others."

Terrance made his way to the counter while Armando went to the back to turn on the music. A few moments later John Coltrane flooded the café, and Armando stepped out of the back and made his way to the front counter. He opened the pink box, pulled a large blueberry muffin out and set it on a plate in front of Terrance. "I think this'll go well with that Ethiopian." He said, grabbing a large paper cup, and sliding it across the counter next to the plate.

Terrance reached into his pocket and pulled out two crumbled bills; gave them a quick straightening, and then handed them to Armando.

He picked up the plate with the muffin on it and turned around, making his way to the airpot on the counter behind him.

"So what's your plan for the day T-Bone?" Armando asked from behind him as he had begun to push the lever on the top of the pot, filling his cup with the freshly brewed coffee.

"Ah, you know; gotta get some work in. Joe ain't been doin' too hot the last couple days, so I figured I'd try and get some aspirin or somethin' for him. Don't need another one of my friends dyin' on me; too hard to find good ones these days."

"Speaking of friends," Armando said into the pastry case while putting a tray of croissants on the bottom shelf, "your little skateboarder buddy stopped by yesterday. He left something for you. Almost forgot."

"Oh, Danny." Terrance said, stirring the sugar into his coffee.

"Yeah, Danny." Armando replied, stepping over to the cash register to pull open the drawer beneath it.

"Here you go," he said, setting a cassette tape on the counter. "It's an old Clash tape."

"Clash?" Terrance asked.

"Yeah, old punk rock band from the seventies." Armando said, stepping back to the pastry case. "You never hear The Clash?"

"He keeps saying I need to expand my musical horizons," Terrance responded with a smile, tilting his head to send his words over his shoulder.

He placed a top onto his cup and turned around to walk back to the counter.

He reached out, grabbed the tape and slid it into his shirt pocket.

"You know I'm gonna get you back for all these coffee's one day right?" he said, causing Armando to stand up and smile at him from behind the case.

"I know T-Bone, and one day, I'm gonna hold you to that as well."

Terrance smiled and then turned around, shouting, "Have a good one," as he made his way outside.

"You too man!" he heard Armando say loudly as the door closed behind him.

He sat down at the table on the patio and peeled the paper wrapper from the base of the muffin and began to systematically pull pieces from it, eating it slowly, savoring every bite, and washing it down with sips of hot coffee.

After a few minutes his muffin was finished. He stood up, slid his chair in and then started making his way back up Sunset to his work spot. It was already beginning to get hot, and he wanted to reach *quota* before the noon sun set in and he was forced to call it quits. He needed to make an extra five bucks today in order to cover the bottle of generic aspirin for Joe. He didn't believe in stealing like many of the other guys did. *"Just cause we're broke, don't mean we have to be thieves,"* he'd say. He already had to deal with security following him through stores, and clerks staring at him, watching his every move, being African-American in North Carolina in the fifties had been a very similar experience for him, so he was already accustomed to the treatment. Most people automatically assumed that he was stealing, but one of his secret pleasures was proving them wrong when he made his way to the front with the merchandise, and pulled out the money to pay for it. He wanted them to feel stupid every time he put his money on the counter. He knew that most of the time they didn't, but he hoped.

* * *

Terrance spent the morning making his money between green lights. He'd wait for the light to turn red, and then make his way to the line between the cars and walk up and down, accepting change and crumpled bills from people on their morning commute.

By noon he had already made close to twenty dollars; enough for lunch, a decent dinner, and a bottle of aspirin and canned soup for his friend. He even pondered spending a few dollars on a bottle of spiced rum to help him celebrate his birthday in style.

He made his way to the Right Aid, grabbed his friend's medicine and then headed back to his house.

When he arrived, he tapped on the side of Joe's tent.

"Hey Joe, you in there?" He called out.

There was a cough from inside the tent, and then a choked response followed by more coughing. "Uh... Yeah."

"Got somethin' for ya," Terrance said. "Open up."

He heard rustling inside the tent, and then the zipper made its way downward, and Joe's dirty, wrinkled face peered out through squinted eyes.

"I picked this up for ya' on the way here." Terrance said, sticking his arm out with a plastic bag in his hand. "It's not much, but I hope it helps. You didn't sound so good so I figured, what they hey."

Joe reached out and took the bag delicately from Terrance. "Whatchu got here?" he asked.

"Ah, not much," Terrance replied. "Just some soup and a bottle of aspirin. Maybe it can help with the cough."

Joe smiled big and toothless, then looked up at Terrance and said, "Thanks T-Bone, Feelin' better already."

"Well that's just fine then," Terrance said, returning the smile. "Well, I gotta gather my laundry; you got anything you need washed, I'm gonna hit the laundromat?"

"Oh, I'm ok," Joe replied, "Thanks though."

"You got it Joe," Terrance said, sending another smile. "You take care of yourself now you hear? And don't forget to take that aspirin you hear."

"Yesir," Joe replied with a cough before zipping the tent back up.

Terrance went inside his house and filled his backpack with his dirty clothes and the blanket that he used as padding on top of the cardboard in his tent, then he made his way to the laundromat, where he relaxed and listened to the Clash tape his young friend had given him on the old Walkman he'd picked up from Goodwill a few months prior.

After his laundry finished up he folded his clothes, filled his backpack and made his way back to the park for some late afternoon bird watching.

He sat on a bench on the side farthest from the boat house, punk rock infused reggae filling his ears with a sound he had never before heard. He sat there, lightly tapping his feet to the rhythm and watching the birds fly lazily back and forth; the giant fountain of water spraying upwards on the other side of the lake as flocks of ducks floated across the surface near the bank.

It was after about an hour that he realized the sun was beginning its daily descent. He checked his watch and it was five-thirty, time for him to make his way to McDonalds, and then back to his house for the night.

He had a routine, and he liked to stick to it. It wasn't the importance of the things that made up his routine; it was the fact that he had one that he felt helped him keep his sanity. *"Once you lose focus on life, it's as good as over for ya,"* he's tell Danny from time to time.

An hour later he had a full stomach, and was quietly playing solitaire in his house, waiting for the sounds of traffic to die down so he could comfortably fall asleep. Another hour went by before his eyes finally fell closed.

* * *

Terrance found himself sitting in a small park, overlooking what he instantly recognized as the San Francisco Bay. He could see the iconic Golden Gate Bridge standing a short ways off, and the island of Alcatraz to his right. It was early afternoon and the smell of salt water was drifting through the air.

Terrance took in a deep breath while admiring how beautifully contrasted the reddish bridge was against the clear blue sky, and silver streaked water. He heard a boat sound its horn in the distant harbor, and felt a smile begin to tug at his cheeks. It had been many years since he had been to San Fran, but it was still the same as it was when his wife and son had been here with him all those years ago, when his family had still been the center of his life.

He stood up and began to make his way to the large wooden observation deck when he saw a flock of birds rising into the air from across the bay, followed by another, and then another. Soon the sky was filled with thousands of birds, all of them making their way frantically south.

They began to fly overhead, the unimaginably large flock, all soaring in the same direction, flapping their wings furiously, a chorus of shrieks and whistles accompanying them. Then Terrance began to notice the small sparks of light. It was only one or two to begin with, but by the time he realized what it was, it had started happening throughout the flock, from one edge of the bay to the other. The birds were igniting, going up in puffs of flame and smoke, falling like tiny pieces of burning origami from the sky.

Terrance watched as streaks of burning carrion fell from above, raining ash and charred feathers on the surface below. Moments later the heat began.

It was just as it had been before; first the tallest of the trees igniting, followed by a blinding light. He heard the screams of those around him, and as he brought his arm up to his face, he saw the strands holding the bridge together begin to snap as the heat melted the tops of the spires away. His sleeve started to smoke as the fabric covering his arm began to melt away, and just as the searing heat began to penetrate the skin across the back of his forearm he awoke, once more covered in sweat, his throat dry, and his pulse racing so strongly that he feared that at his age, he was having a heart attack.

He lay there staring at the ceiling of his tent while the world around him came flooding back, his hand pressed firmly against his chest. First it was the cool air, followed by the sounds of cars rushing by overhead replacing the piercing ringing in his ears.

He took a long shuddered breath, lying there while going through a mental checklist of the symptoms of heart attack and stroke. When he realized that his pulse was slowly beginning to descend, he threw the sleeping bag that was covering him aside and let the cool night air once again wash over his body.

"My God," he whispered to himself in the dark.

Revelations

His memory was freshly awash with a swirling vortex of fiery birds falling from the sky, and the smell of scorched earth and burnt fowl.

He was trembling, and he realized that he had must have started to cry again because he had a thin line of moisture running down his cheek past his ear, and there was a small wet spot on his pillow.

He brought his hands up and ran his fingers through his hair. As his palms graced his forehead he felt the thick layer of sweat that had beaded up smear across.

He reached to his right and grabbed the bottle of water that he kept next to him in the tent and unscrewed the top; leaning over to take a heavy drink of the liquid, then remembered the bottle of rum he had bought and fished it out of his backpack. The bottle glinted in his hands as he ran his fingers around the textured rivets of the cap. He held it for a minute before taking another deep breath and putting it back in his bag, taking another sip of water and then collapsing back down again.

He pressed the backlight button on his Indiglo wristwatch, and then brought his arm up in front of him to read the time through the sapphire light; it read 3:52 A.M.

He let his arm fall back down, and lay there, revisiting the two dreams over and over until the pair seemed to blend with each other. His body still tingled, and for the next hour or so he stared at the ceiling, his eyes dilated in the darkness before sleep eventually found him and pulled him back.

Thursday the 20th

When Terrance awoke again he yawned and stretched his arms out, folding his hands at the wrists as they contacted with the wall behind him. He held it for a moment and then brought his hands back down to rub his face and wipe the sleep from his eyes.

He heard Joe cough next door, and lay there for a moment before calling out, "Feelin' better Joe?"

There was another cough, and then Joe responded with, "I'm still alive."

Terrance smiled, and then pulled himself up into the seated position. He reached down and grabbed his sleeping bag, folded it neatly, and set it against the side of the tent. He leaned forward, grabbed his backpack and pulled it towards him. The zipper hummed lightly as he pulled it to the bottom and reached in, his hand retreating from the bag with a clean pair of socks, and a fresh t-shirt. He only had two pairs of pants, and he would joke about the fact that *you ain't supposed to wash denim that often anyways,* using it as his excuse not to worry about washing them too frequently. He'd usually wait until he could smell them beginning to take on the *funk* before he'd add them to his wash load.

He slipped the shirt over his head, put on the clean pair of socks and pulled his boots on before climbing out onto the porch. He had no sooner bent down to zip his house up, when sirens blasted, and three black, unmarked SUV's pulled a small white car over in front of him.

In an instant the porch was alive with activity. There were police jumping out of their vehicles with guns drawn, and a cop on the loudspeaker telling the driver and passengers of the white car to put their hands out of the windows.

One of the police officers told Terrance to get back, and since he had seen this type of thing erupt into gunfire in the past, he decided it best if he didn't stick around; he would be able to get the full story with moment by moment details from Joe later.

He made his way quickly down to Temple Street, and then cut left towards Echo Park. He was a little hungry, and he figured since it was his sixty-fifth birthday, he'd treat himself to a nice breakfast.

He made his way up to a little diner on the corner of Sunset and Park and sat down in the outside patio. After a few minutes a waiter in skinny jeans and a low cut V-neck shirt walked out, his wool knit cap sitting like a yamaka on the back of his head, and said, "Excuse me, but you can't hang out here, the patio is for customers only so uh, you're gonna have to leave or I'm gonna be forced to call the police."

Terrance looked at him and began to say, "I just want to have breakfast," when the snotty waiter turned his back and walked quickly back inside.

Terrance let his head drop slightly, feeling all too familiar tinge of embarrassment seeping in, and then stood up, pushed his chair in, and made his way to the Burrito King on the corner, where he ordered a breakfast burrito with everything in it, a large coffee, and just because it was his celebration, a glass of orange juice.

He sat on one of the street-side stools and enjoyed his breakfast, relishing the amazing food, and the hot cup of coffee. When he finished, he walked back to the counter, placed a dollar in the tip jar, said thank you to the worker and made his way into the smoke shop next door where he bought a single Black and Mild to help kick off his birthday the right way, "With a good breakfast, and a fine cigar."

He walked down Sunset, puffing on his Black and Mild and sipping his coffee as he made his way to the Tropical to say good morning to Armando.

When he arrived he saw Tony Pony hanging out on the patio. Tony was another *down on his luck* individual who stayed in the Silverlake area. He was an older cat, and due to years of heroin and meth use was extremely skinny, and had the attention span of a squirrel with ADHD.

Terrance walked up and, and as he approached, Tony called out loudly to the empty street, "Look everybody, It's T-Bone Williams, the man of the hour!"

"Hey Tony. How you doin' man?" Terrance asked.

"Good, good. Hey, I was just thinking about this. Anybody ever call you pork chop? You know, cause your name's T-Bone, so it's kinda like the same right?"

He scratched his head and let his gaze fall to the ground below, when something in the gutter caught his eye, and he moved forward to inspect it closer.

"Alright Tony, you have a good one man, stay up," Terrance said as he walked past to stick his head in the door of the Tropical to say hi to his friend.

"Armando?" He called out, when a young Hispanic girl stuck her head out of the back.

"Sorry T-Bone," she responded, her accent dancing across the space between them. "Armando had to take the day off, it's just me here today."

"Oh hi, Lucy." Terrance said. "It's ok, you're prettier to look at anyways."

She smiled really big. "Oh you get out of here you old flirt," and pretended like she was going to throw a paper cup at him.

"Alright, alright, I'm leaving, no need to get violent."

She smiled again and called out as he was turning to leave, "Have a good day T-Bone."

He waved over his shoulder and replied, "Will do," as he once again hit the street.

"Hey man," Tony said loudly as Terrance was about to hit the corner.

"What's up Tony?" he asked.

"You ain't got a dollar I can get do you? Even just a quarter?"

Terrance shook his head and rolled his eyes, then walked back to his acquaintance.

"Man, you know I'm broke too right? You're lucky it's my birthday." He said as he handed him a folded dollar bill.

"Thanks man thanks." Tony responded, instantly turning his attention to a dog that was walking across the street.

Terrance heard him calling out, "Here puppy puppy," as he turned the corner, and once again let a small shake of his head emphasize the humor he found in Tony's presence. He made his way down Sunset to what the locals referred to as *The Junction*; a small strip about three blocks long, with a collection of shops that represented Silverlake in its heyday, and some newer ones that showed the hip, trendy side it was trying to become.

He passed the ninety-nine cent store, and paused, pondering over getting a candy bar, but then remembered the rather large cavity he had in one of his back teeth, and the ensuing pain he would endure as the overly sweet chocolate worked its way into the hole.

'One of these days I'll get that looked at.'

He had said these words more times than he could remember, but had still never made his way to the clinic to get it taken care of.

He decided on ice cream instead. There was something about the cold that didn't cause pain from the sugar. He figured one of the people at the fancy coffee shop down the street would know where the best ice cream was; he hadn't bought anything that wasn't from Rite Aid in so long, he had no idea anymore, and he had already passed the Baskin Robins. He figured he'd grab some ice cream, and maybe catch the bus to the beach for the day. It was his birthday after all.

He approached the café, and walked up to one of the patrons sitting at a table in the front, their face buried in a laptop. He walked up and said, "Excuse me?"

They ignored him.

"Excuse me, you mind if I ask you a question?"

"Look man, the guy said, yanking his gaze away from his computer screen, "I don't have change all right, now leave me alone, I'm trying to get some work done. You know what that is right, work? What real people do?"

Terrance stood there for a moment, embarrassment flooding through him as he looked back at the man's eyes staring in disgust from beneath the wide brim of the Amish style hat he wore.

"I'm sorry man, I just wanted to know where I could find some good ice cream around here," he said in a conquered tone.

"Yeah," the guy snapped, sarcasm smearing across his face, "and I said, fuck off."

Terrance felt a tear beginning to tug its way into the corner of his eye. He paused, his stomach knotting tightly and then whispered, "Well, thanks anyways," before turning to make his way down to Santa Monica Boulevard.

He heard the guy with the computer sneer, "Whatever man," as he was walking away, and he had to tell himself, *'It's not his fault, he didn't know I wasn't trying to beg for change. He was probably just having a bad day.'*

He walked a few blocks down and grabbed a seat on the bus bench. Ten minutes later the 4 came rolling up, and Terrance climbed aboard, making his way to the back of the rows, grabbing an empty seat next to a window.

It had been months since he had been to the beach, and he looked forward to lying down in the sand and listening to the waves crash along the shore. He knew he'd have to walk a good ways down the beach so the police wouldn't harass him about "sleeping on the beach". The last time he had come to Santa Monica he had almost been arrested because the police had rolled up on him and told him he had to leave. He had tried to explain that he was just spending the day on the beach like everyone else, but the cops had a different view of it, and told him if he didn't leave, they'd charge him with trespassing and take him to jail.

He sat on the bus watching the city go by, and people getting on and off the bus. Two hours later he was stepping off the bus in Santa Monica. The ocean spread out in front of him, stretching into the horizon with the cool salted breeze wafting lazily past.

He immediately made for pier, and then down to the sand, where he took off his shoes and socks, rolled his pant legs up and began his trek up the beach to where there were less people. He walked for quite a while before finding a place he felt comfortable settling into, and then laid down, propped his head up on his arms, and watched the waves roll in and out for the next two hours, listening to the symphony of ocean sounds and gulls.

He was on the beach for about two hours, and hadn't realized that he had closed his eyes. When he opened them up, he was standing back at the pier, and the early afternoon sun was beating down upon him.

He stood at the beginning of the amusement filled structure, wondering how he had gotten back there when he realized that once again, he was dreaming. It was just as real as the other two had been, and he felt the impending sense that something bad was going to happen.

He could hear the waves crashing, and the sound of the rollercoaster as it clanked its way to the top, and the screams of the people as it rushed downwards and into a loop. He turned his head and watched as people made their way to and from on the boardwalk, some on skateboards, some riding bikes, and countless more walking up and down it.

Revelations

There were people laughing, and children holding balloons and cotton candy, and everywhere he looked people were smiling and having fun. Then he saw the steam.

It was as if the ocean was beginning to rise towards the sky. There was a layer of mist forming, and steam began to rise from the surface of the water. He turned to look at the beach and saw that the wet part of the sand where it contacted with the waves had evaporated, and as the water pulled back, it left no visible marks, drying up instantly.

The sound of a balloon popping ripped his attention away from the beach and he saw a little boy crying with a deflated piece of red rubber attached to a string at his feet. That's when the people that had cranked to the top of the rollercoaster began to scream again, but this time it wasn't from fear or the thought of the quick loops and fast turns, it was from pain. It was loud and primal, guttural and sharp.

He felt the heat, and watched as the restaurant at the end of the pier started to smoke, and the roof combusted, sending flames into the scorching air.

The last thing he saw as he looked past the sea of burning hair and melting skin was the ocean boiling like a pot left on the stove too long. Then his breath in his lungs turned to flame.

* * *

He shot awake, and was sitting upright almost instantly. The sun had already started to go below the horizon, and an evening chill had set into the air. He could feel the soft sting of sunburn that had crept across his skin and realized that he was sweating again. Each time he had one of these dreams it began to feel more and more real. There was an unsettling feeling that had begun to sink into him, that the dreams were much more than just that, like they were visions of things that were going to happen; premonitions.

Revelations

He brought himself to his feet, and tried to shake off the feeling that they were more than just vivid nightmares, but no matter how hard he tried, there was that feeling in the back of his mind that was screaming for him to get ready for those things to happen, that the earth was going to burn, and that it was *his* job to tell the world, that *he* had been somehow, chosen, to relay the message of impending apocalypse.

As he made his way back down the beach, the waves crashing loudly against the shore, his mind continued to race.

He had feared from the moment he had ended up on the street, with no options and nowhere to go that he would end up like the other homeless people; alone and talking to themselves on a street corner somewhere, not even capable of writing a typical "hungry, need food" sign. Now here he was entertaining the idea that he was having psychic visions of the end of the world, and that he was being charged with saving humanity.

He made his way back down the beach, and sat quietly the entire bus ride back to Silver Lake. He felt like he was carrying a bag of mossy stones in his stomach, and his mind kept replaying the images from his dreams over and over.

When he reached his tent he crawled inside and pulled the bottle of rum out of his bag, hesitating slightly before twisting the cap free with a series of satisfying clicks that signaled the seal had been broken, and the warming liquid inside was available.

He took a long swig off the bottle, screwed the cap back on and let himself fall backwards onto the blanket, his head landing with a soft thud into the folded jacket he used as a pillow.

He lay there for another few hours, his mind going over and over the events before finally, he dozed off. The last thing he thought as his mind began to fade, and the sounds of the outside world drifted farther and farther away was, *'Please don't let me dream.'*

Friday the 21st

Terrance woke up the following morning feeling refreshed. The first thought that went through his head was, *'Thank God I didn't have another one of those dreams.'*

He stretched, got dressed, and made his way outside.

As he stepped out the saw Joe walking towards him down the sidewalk.

"How you doin' Joe? You feelin' any better?" he asked, bending down to zip his house up.

"Had to piss real bad, but I think I'm doin' a touch better. Headache gone."

"That's good," Terrance replied with a smile, reaching out to tap Joe on the shoulder.

Joe nodded, and then added, "Can't stay sick forever, gots to get back ta work. Man gotta eat."

"Heard that!" Terrance said, marking it down in his mental notepad to pick up another can of soup for Joe. "Well, you take care now ya hear," he said, turning to make his way back up to Sunset for his morning walk.

He had strolled down to Tropical, and was standing inside, enjoying his coffee, and carrying on some light conversation with Armando, when the sound of a skateboard approaching grabbed his attention. He heard the distinct click sound it made when someone stepped hard on the tail to get it to pop into their hands, and saw the door start to open.

"Hey T-Bone," the voice said, immediately followed by a skinny teenage kid with shoulder length, scraggly blonde hair. "What's up Armando?" the kid said with a smile, flipping a sideways peace sign in the air as he did.

"Hey Danny," Armando called out from behind the counter, "Coffee?"

"Hell yeah, you don't think I just came here to see this old bastard do ya?"

He tapped Terrance's arm as he walked past, making a B-line directly for the cup that was being set on the counter.

"What'd I say about having to beat some respect into you?" Terrance asked with a grin.

Danny grabbed his cup and turned to make his way to the airpot full of steaming brew. "Good luck old man," he said, flinching towards him as he walked past, "might wanna bring some friends."

Terrance laughed, and Armando called from behind the counter, "Always talkin' shit man."

Danny smiled as he set his skateboard against the coffee station, and pumped the lever to fill his cup.

"Where you been T-Bone? I haven't seen you in a few days, I was startin' to worry, thought you might have gone and died on me," Danny said while dumping a rather large amount of sugar into his coffee.

"Nah, I ain't dead yet." Terrance replied. "Besides, I can't leave, then there'd be nobody to keep your little punk ass in line."

Danny laughed and then picked up his skateboard, wanna grab a seat for a while? I got the day off from school, some dead guy's birthday or something."

"You mean President's day?" Terrance said, nodding to shoot smile to Armando, and sticking his hand up to say good-bye.

"You two stay outta trouble," Armando called out as they left.

Danny grabbed the table closest to the corner facing the street, and Terrance sat down across from him.

"Did you get the tape I left you?" Danny asked. "I was at Canterbury in Pasadena the other day and saw it. I thought about you, cause you're the only person on the planet that still uses a Walkman with cassettes. Figured you'd like it, it's one of my favorite albums."

"I did. I listened to it till my batteries died. That was really nice of you Danny, thanks."

"So…" Danny started, pausing to take a sip of his coffee, "you doing all right T-Bone?"

Terrance gave him a puzzled look and responded, "Yeah, why you askin like that?"

"Well, don't take this personal or anything, but you kinda look like shit. You're not usin' dope like those other idiots you run around with are you, cause I'll kick your ass if I find out you are. Don't want you dyin' from an overdose in an alley somewhere."

"No! No Danny, I'm not using. Think I wanna end up like old Tony? *Uh-uhh…* Not me boy." He paused. "Just ain't been sleepin' to good these past few nights. Keep having these *really* bad dreams."

"Your family?" Danny asked, trying not to be too invasive.

"No. It's stranger than that. It's like, I fall asleep, but then I wake up, and I'm in a different place every time, but the same thing keeps happening. First it starts to get bright outside, then everything above the trees starts to burn, then the trees catch fire, and then eventually everything around me is burnin', people, houses, everything. And it's real too man, I mean, it feels *real*. Every time I wake up, I look down expecting to see smoke."

"Wow," Danny said, now staring intently at Terrance from across the table. "Then what?"

"Nothin'," Terrance answered, "It's just that. Heat, then burning and fire, and soon as I'm bout to go up myself, I wake up."

"How long have you been having these dreams?" Danny asked.

"Bout the last three days now." Terrance answered. "Seems every time I fall asleep I have one."

Danny took another sip from his cup.

"I went to the beach yesterday," Terrance continued, "took a walk along the sand to enjoy my birthday, and.."

"It was your birthday!?" Danny interrupted. "You should have told me man, I would have gotten you something."

"It's fine, didn't exactly have much of a celebration."

"Still," Danny said, "You gotta tell me when it's your birthday, I coulda got you cake or something."

"Oh, it's ok. Thanks though."

"Ok," Danny continued, "You were saying about the beach? Sorry, but you didn't tell me about your birthday. You gotta tell me these things man, you're my friend, and friends get shit for their friends on their birthdays."

Terrance smiled.

"Now you were saying about the beach?"

Terrance nodded. "So yeah, went to the beach,"

"Can't believe you didn't tell me your birthday was coming up," Danny interrupted with a whisper, and shake of his head.

"and decided to take me a stroll. Ended up walking a ways down, and falling asleep. It was the same thing; Santa Monica catching fire. One moment I'm laying on the sand, listening to the waves crashing, next moment, I'm standing at the entrance to the pier, and the entire thing begins to burn." He paused, taking a sip from his cup. "You know, every dream is the same. It's like the sky is catching on fire, like the heats coming from up there," he said, his eyes moving up to the clouds, "it's hard to explain, but I keep getting this feeling like something really bad's gonna happen."

"Damn," Danny responded, not exactly knowing what to think about what he was hearing. "Maybe you're having like premonitions or something, like seeing into the future; things that haven't happened yet, but will?"

"Nah," Terrance replied, "I don't believe in that psychic mumbo-jumbo, that's about as real as Santa Clause and the Easter Bunny."

Danny's eyes got really big, and he set his cup down on the table, letting his mouth fall wide open. "Santa Clause isn't real!!?" He asked rather loudly.

Terrance stared at him for a second, and then shook his head, a smile growing across his face and replied, "Oh shut up." He paused. "I'm tryin' ta be serious here."

"I know," Danny said with a big grin on his face, "I'm just messin' with ya."

He tilted his cup back, finishing the last of his coffee, and then tossed it in the container next to the light pole at the cross walk.

"Two points!" He said, as he picked up his board and stood up. "Hey man, I'm gonna go try and get a session in, it's too nice a day to not be skating. You gonna be around later?"

Terrance nodded, "Yeah, I'll be around."

"Cool," Danny said, turning to drop his deck to the ground, "I'll catch you later then."

He kicked the board forward, waved to Armando and then took two quick steps

51

before jumping on to the moving board and skating off.

Terrance sat there for a minute before finishing his coffee, and then deciding to make his way to work. It was Friday, and that meant people were usually pretty generous; in a good mood because the week was over, or they were getting ready to go out and barbeque, or whatever it was that they did. And it was a three-day weekend apparently, which meant extra generous.

He stood up and waved to Armando who waved back, and then headed up the street to go to work.

By two o'clock he had made close to forty dollars, and decided to grab himself, and the other guys a big bag of McDonalds cheeseburgers. They were only a buck, and with what he'd made today, him and the fellas could eat like kings. He even considered pulling the rest of his rum out and giving it a pass around.

* * *

Revelations

By the time evening had set in, Terrance, Guitar Joe, Mad Dog, and Jimmy had filled their guts, and were sitting up on a flat spot on the side of the overpass playing rummy. They were listening to the radio off of an old battery powered boom box Mad Dog had found a couple weeks earlier and chatting amongst themselves, the soft roar of the freeway permeating the air around them.

Terrance had dumped the rest of his birthday rum into the large Coca Cola cup that they had been passing around the table for the last few games. By this point everyone had gotten a full stomach, and a nice buzz on.

"So you're tellin' me, that the fool that owns goodwill is a multi millionaire?" Jimmy asked, setting down a run on the cardboard box they were using as a table.

"Hell yeah he is." Mad Dog replied. "Think about it. Their entire business is reselling stuff that is given to them fo' free. They don't pay fo' shit, it's all donations. So then, they fill their stores, sell the shit that they don't pay a dime for in the first place, and then pay their employees minimum wage, and offer no benefits. And the *only* reason he hires people like us to work there, is because the gov'ment gives him a tax break fo' hiring broke ass mufukkas like us. It's a scam, and that guys laughing his rich ass straight to the bank." He paused, reaching out and taking a sip out of the cup. "That's why when I *really* need sumpin', and I haven't found shit in the bins, I make my way over to St. Vincent on San Fernando. At least that way, I'm giving my money to an organization that actually helps people." He scoffed. "Goodwill. They can kiss my white ass..."

"We got Saint Christopher over here homie." Jimmy said sarcastically. "Saving the world one dirty pair of chonies at a time."

"Yo dawg, it's better than putting wood on the fire," Mad Dog replied.

"Speakin of fire, who gots a lighter?" Joe asked.

"Depends," Mad Dog replied, "What you sparkin' up over there?"

"Oh, you know. Got me a bag of snipes, gon' twist a smoke."

"Aiight," Mad Dog replied, "Kick it, I be right back, think I got one in my house."

He got up and made his way down the embankment towards his tent, yelling over his shoulder as he did, "And don't go eyefuckin' my cards either."

The guys at the table smiled as Joe slowly pulled his hand back.

"I'll know if you looked!" He yelled, unzipping his front door as he did.

Two minutes later he was back at the table sliding a lighter across the cardboard to Joe who had spread out a small handful of cigarette butts, and was rolling the burnt tobacco out of them into a small pile in front of him. He dropped the used tobacco into a rolling paper and rolled it with careless precision, then sparked it and leaned back, exhaling a large puff of stale smoke.

"You know those things are gonna kill you right?" Terrance said, making a statement more than a question.

"Who want's to live forever?" Joe replied flatly.

"Don't know about ya'll, but I got plenty of livin' left to do." Mad Dog responded. "Hell, can't die till I get with one of them fine as Armenian girls you see hangin' out at the Starbucks on Hollywood and Western; and to do that, I need money, which means I can't die till I'm paid." He looked back and forth between the others, then extended his arms outwards and smiled really big, "So looks like I'm gonna be here for a mad minute."

The group laughed.

"Mad Dog, You're a fool homie, you know that?" Jimmy said with a smile.

"All right fellas," Terrance said, laying a set of three 7's down, and putting his last card face down on the pile, "Think I'm gonna turn in for the night."

They nodded; slapped hands, and then Terrance started making his way down the dirt incline towards his house.

"Oh, and Happy Birthday T-Bone!" Joe called out down the hill.

"Oh shit! It's your birthday T-Bone?" Jimmy called out, "Happy birthday homie!"

"Birthday was yesterday," he called back up the hill, "but thanks fellas."

"Yeah," Mad Dog yelled, "happy birthday you old fool."

Terrance smiled as he unzipped the door to his house. The guys he considered his close buddy's might have been a bit crazy to most people, but to him they were the closest things he had to friends.

He settled into his house, kicked off his shoes and placed them near the entrance with his socks folded nicely inside them. He pulled his jacket off and folded it up, laying it at the top of his blanket, and then took off his belt and set it to his right.

He lay there for quite some time, staring at the picture of his family before finally drifting off to sleep. When he opened his eyes, he could hear them talking in the background.

* * *

Terrance found himself sitting at what had used to be his kitchen table. The television was playing from the living room, and he could hear his wife yelling up to their son.

"T.J., get your but down here, you're gonna be late for school."

Terrance Junior; it was her idea. "Continuing a legacy," she had said.

'Some legacy...'

His eyes poured over the room. Many of the things he remembered were still in their place, but there was something different about the house, something new.

His eyes wandered to the walls, and he realized that the kitchen was a different color; no longer the vibrant yellow they had picked while standing pregnant at the home depot all those years ago. It was now a light blue, with a thin purple trim, and the cabinets had been replaced with stained wood.

"I said, hurry up!" he heard her yell.

"Tish?" he called out, barely above a whisper.

His wife's name was Latisha, but he called her Tish for short; had since he met her in high school.

"There's been unusually high solar activity lately," the voice coming from the T.V. said.

"Mom, You seen my headphones?" his son called out from upstairs.

"First off," she replied in a stern tone, "it's *have you* seen my headphones, and no, I haven't. And besides, you don't need your headphones at school anyways; you should be spending your free time studying so you can go to college, and not end up flipping burgers down the street."

"It's August 28th, and boy is it warm out."

"Ain't that the truth Bill? I haven't seen a summer this hot in as long as I can remember.

Terrance started to get up when a flash through the kitchen window caught his eye.

A little ways across town Terrance saw smoke starting to rise into the sky, and saw swarms of birds beginning to take flight.

"No. No, no, no..." He said as he attempted to pull his gaze from the window and make his way in the direction of the living room.

"Tish! Tish, where are you?"

He came to the living room but no one was there.

"T.J.?" He shouted, "We have to get out of here, now!"

He heard something heavy drop on the second floor, where the bedrooms were.

"Latisha! We have to go, now!"

He darted to the stairs, and took them three at a time, then stopped dead in his tracks as his eyes made contact with the door at the end of the hallway, the closed door that blocked what used to be his room; their room. There was smoke coming from underneath it, curling slowly upwards, a thin trail of black and grey tendrils, reaching towards the ceiling.

"Tish." He said, his voice cracking as tears began forming at the rim of his eyelids. "T.J."

He started slowly moving down the hall, the clouding air beginning to sting his eyes, and sweat beginning to bead across his forehead as the temperature around him rose.

"Please no," he whispered as he reached out and grabbed the scalding doorknob, yanking it open to a fiery blast from the inferno it had held contained inside.

He shot awake, catching himself screaming, and falling immediately into a fit of hysteric sobbing.

His body was shaking, and his mind was being torn apart with the guilt of not being able to save his family.

He sat and sobbed. There was no respite in the pain that he was feeling, no escaping the vision that had been burned into his mind, the smell of burning wood and flesh; the loss of his family.

"Hey T-Bone? You alright in there man?"

He heard the voices, but they sounded distant, miles away from the agony he was surrounded by.

"Get outta the way Joe."

His mind replayed the event over and over, and just as the zipper to his house started to work its way downward, it hit him.

'August 28th. That's when it's gonna happen!'

The flap pulled backwards, and when Terrance's eyes focused on the movement, he saw Mad Dog's face peering inside.

"You ok in there dawg?" He asked. "Sounded like you was bein murdered in there."

Terrance took a deep breath, shuddering as he released the warm air, and brought his hands up to his face, wiping away the salty trails his tears had made from his eyes down to his chest. He rubbed his left hand shakily across his cheeks, his body shivering as his hand dropped to his side.

"You need me to flag someone down; get you an ambalance or somethin'?"

"No...," he replied, his voice shaking as bad as his body. "No, I'm fine, I'll be fine, thanks though Mad Dog."

"Ok, well, if'n you need anythin' we right here for you my nig. We ain't goin' nowhere, just holla' aiight?"

Terrance nodded.

August 28th.

"Thanks Mad Dog."

"You're welcome man." He said, backing out and zipping his door back up.

He could hear Joe and the others asking if he was alright, and what had happened.

He sat there, still dazed from the vision as Mad Dog explained to the others that it was just a bad dream, that he was fine, and for everyone to give him some space, and go to back to bed.

August 28th. He kept replaying the date over and over in his head. Somehow he knew that's when it was going to happen, but what he didn't know, was what he was supposed to do about it.

He lay there for the rest of the night, going over scenario after scenario, waiting for the sun to rise, so that he could talk to the only person who might be able to help him; Danny. He knew that Danny was still in school, and might have a professor or someone he could ask about solar activity. He knew that he was adept at using the internet; something he had never gotten the luxury of learning. He knew somehow, that he could help.

Saturday the 22nd

When the sun was finally bright enough to spread its glow into his house, Terrance brought his wrist up and read the time; 10:34, *'Time to go.'*

He got ready and started making his way to the Tropical. Twenty minutes later he was heading down Sunset when he saw a group of younger people standing in front of the 7-11. He approached and said, "Excuse me."

One of them turned and quickly responded with, "We don't have any change, sorry man."

"That's not what I was gonna ask," Terrance continued, "Could one of you tell me what day it is?"

The guy that had spoken to him just stared at him blankly and then scoffed. "This guy..."

One of the girls pulled her phone out, glanced at it and then said, "Sunday."

"No, what's the *date* today?"

She looked at him puzzled for a second, and then smiled, responding, "Oh, the twenty-second."

"Thank you," he said, turning to continue on his way to the café.

'The twenty-second... Dear God, we only have less than a week left...'

Another twenty minutes later and he arrived at the Tropical. He stuck his head in, and Armando gave his usual, "Good Morning T-Bone."

Terrance replied with a head nod.

"Have you seen Danny this morning?" he asked.

"Not yet, why, you lookin' for him?" Armando responded from the back.

"Yeah, it's kind of important."

He paused as he turned to leave, then turned back around and added, "Hey, if you see him, could you tell him I need to talk to him, and that it's *very* important? I'll be at the new library up the street."

"You got it," Armando called out as the door was closing shut.

Revelations

Terrance headed back up Sunset, his eyes moving to the palm trees that lined the street, the vision of them igniting putting an extra incentive to quicken his pace.

Ten minutes later he arrived at the Edendale branch library, his legs shaking and sweat working its way down his back.

As he stepped in, the quiet air-conditioned atmosphere wrapped itself around him. He made his way to the information desk, waited for the woman to finish her quiet phone call, and then asked politely where he could find books on solar activity.

She looked at him suspiciously for a moment, and then told him, "If we have any, they'd be under in the scientific section; back wall to the left."

He said, "Thank you," and then turned to make his way to the section.

For the next two hours he poured over book after book, looking for solar activity, but coming up with everything from solar power, to sunspots; nothing that could cause the end of the world, and the sun wasn't going to explode any time soon.

He was running out of patience, and the frustration had begun to reach its boiling point when he felt a hand come to rest on his shoulder.

"T-Bone."

Terrance jumped nearly out of his skin, spinning sideways in his chair, and leaning back as he did so.

"Jesus Christ on a crutch."

"Sorry," Danny said, standing just in front of him, "Armando said you were looking for me; said you'd be here and that it was important."

Terrance took a deep breath and exhaled sharply, then tapped Danny on the arm as he stood up and said, "Let's get outta here, there's somethin' I need to tell you about."

They were walking towards the park when Terrance started the conversation up.

"Look, like I told you earlier, I've been having these really bad dreams lately, real bad. It's like I'm actually in them, but I can't do anything about it, like I have to watch, and can't stop anything that happens." He paused, pressing the crosswalk signal to cross Glendale into the park. "They started three days ago, and they've been getting worse; *stronger*."

They made it through the intersection and started their way through the park, heading for the benches that were at the backside, furthest away from the people.

"What are they about?" Danny asked, starting to feel slightly concerned for his friend.

"It's the same thing every time, first the air gets really hot, then the birds take to the sky and start to ignite, falling like *fiery rain*, and then the treetops go up. Next thing I know, everything around me is burning, and just as I realize that I'm about to catch fire, I wake up."

Danny stayed quiet, not knowing what to think as he walked along side Terrance.

"And you said it's the same dream every time?" he asked after a moment.

"Well not exactly," Terrance said. "More like the same situation."

They passed the boathouse on their right, and as Terrance glanced inside, he felt a sudden ping of sorrow for the people sitting outside on the patio. He knew they had no idea what was going to happen, and that there would be nothing he could do to save them.

"You see, the first one, I was sittin' at Tropical and I watched all of Sunset catch fire. The next one was San Francisco, and then Santa Monica, and finally last night, I was at my ex-wife's house in North Carolina, clear across the country; but it was the same thing, the birds, the treetops, the heat."

Danny stayed quiet.

"So I think, whatever's gonna happen, it's gonna happen here in the U.S. And I think I know when it's gonna happen too; August 28th; in one week."

Revelations

Danny glanced at him, before letting his eyes graze the water, peering at a large grey goose for a moment. "T-Bone, I don't mean anything by this, and I'm not saying that I don't believe you, but I have to ask because you're my friend." He paused, trying to formulate the right way to ask before settling on just coming out with it. "You're *sure* you're not using right?"

"What?" Terrance responded surprised, "No! Not at all." He took a deep breath and exhaled sharply. "Look Danny, You know me, you've known me for almost five years now, you know I'm not crazy, and you know I hate drugs. Come on now."

"I know," Danny said, turning his gaze to Terrance, "I just had to ask. This isn't exactly something people come out with everyday you know. You're basically telling me, that your having visions of the world coming to an end, and that it's going to happen in a week. You have to understand why I needed to ask."

Terrance took another deep breath, realizing that it did sound pretty crazy, and almost like something Tony Pony would have made up four weeks into one of his crystal meth binges.

He tapped Danny on the arm, and took a seat at one of the stone benches spaced out across the back of the lake.

They sat quietly for a moment before Danny spoke up. "So what do you think it is?"

"I'm not sure," Terrance replied, "but the dream I had at my ex-wife's house; there was a T.V. playing in the background, and the news man was saying something about high solar activity; whatever that means. That's why I was at the library, I was trying to do some research on ways that solar activity could cause what I'm seeing in my nightmares."

"Solar activity? That could be a million things. You don't have anything a little more specific than that?" Danny asked.

"Sorry," Terrance responded

"All right," Danny said after a moment, "I'll talk to my science professor tomorrow and see what he says, maybe he'll have some more useful information for us, but until then, don't try and go doing anything crazy alright."

Terrance nodded. "Thanks Danny. I knew you'd be able to help."

Danny smiled as he got up. "Well don't hold your breath, cause we haven't found anything out yet." He paused. "Well, I gotta get going. I'll find you at the spot tomorrow."

Terrance nodded, and watched as Danny dropped his skateboard to the ground, and kicked his way down the path, putting his headphones in his ears as he did.

It was still early in the day, but Terrance was already beginning to fear the inevitable nightfall, which would bring darkness, one less day till the 28th, and sleep.

* * *

Donald Morrison

Terrance looked up. He was in a place he'd never seen before. He recognized the language written everywhere; it was Spanish. He could hear Spanish music playing, and people speaking it all around him. He blinked heavily, and then began looking around. Everywhere he looked there was Spanish writing, and then he saw a green and white Volkswagen Bug with a taxicab sign on top of it drive by; and as he glanced at the license plate, he managed to catch the word Mexico.

He walked quickly towards one of the blue newspaper stands near by and scanned the front cover. It had a large blue lock on the front, and simply said, The News, and to his surprise, was written in English. He scanned to the middle, and read the date; August 28th.

He pulled his gaze away from the paper, and looked around at the tens of thousands of people surrounding him; walking, and driving, and biking. He was in the middle of a swarm when he realized what was about to happen.

He began to yell, "You have to get out of here! You're all gonna burn. You have to get to safety."

He ran back and forth, trying to get peoples attention, but every time he tried to grab someone, they'd pause, look right through him, and then continue about their business.

"Please, I'm trying to help you. You're gonna die..."

No one listened to him, and then the brightness began.

He stood in the middle of an intersection, repeating, "You have to leave... You're going to die," until the heat began, and the world around him erupted into flame. He repeated himself until the last person had fallen to the ground, and his skin began to boil, and then he woke up.

There was no screaming this time, no hysterics, just tears. He lay there, not sobbing, but taking deep, labored breaths, and feeling the tears working their way down the side of his face past his ears, ending in a moist puddle on the jacket below his head.

He knew now that he couldn't save the people in his visions, and that for some cruel twist of fate, some foul reason beyond his understanding, that he was cursed to watch the world around him burn, and eventually die, before he himself was consumed in the flames that brought with them the real, waking world he inhabited.

He knew now that they were something more than just dreams; they *were* visions of what was to come, they were revelations.

He brought his hands behind his head and interlocked his fingers, staring through the darkness at the photo on the ceiling of his house. He wanted desperately to tell his ex-wife and son what was going to happen, to warn them about the coming disaster, but since he had been thrown out, she had changed the number, and had a restraining order filed against him. Even if he could contact her, if he did, he'd be sent to jail for it, and he didn't want to spend his last week on earth locked in a cell, with nowhere to go when it all went down. Besides, she wouldn't have believed, or listened to him for that matter anyways, so it would be a waste of his time.

Three more hours went by, and when he looked at his watch it read 9:36. He handled his usual morning routine, zipped the tent, and then made his way up the stairs on the side of the overpass to take a leak.

He stood there, finishing up and wondering if Danny would be there when he got to the café when he heard the tell tale *whoop* sound of a police cruiser flashing its siren, the signal that his morning was about to get interrupted.

"You wanna zip it up and come on down here for a moment," a voice called out from behind him. "We'd like to talk to you for a second."

Terrance finished fastening his belt and turned around to face the officer who had called up to him.

At the bottom of the stairs were two police officers, one a taller white guy, and the other a shorter black man.

'Great, a salt n' pepper team,' he thought as he made his way down the stairs.

He already knew how this was gonna go, so he prepped himself mentally for what he was about to deal with, "Gotta make it go smoothly as possible," he'd say, "The less *nigger* you act, the quicker it's done.

"Morning officers," he said as he approached the bottom of the stairs.

"All right," the white one began, holding his hand out, the other moving to the gun strapped to his side, "that's close enough."

He stopped, two stairs from the bottom.

"Why don't you step on over here and face the wall."

Terrance already knew the drill.

He walked over to the wall where the cop had pointed, and put his nose two inches from it, folding both hands on top of his head, and spreading his legs a little more than shoulder length apart.

"You wanna tell us what you were doing up there?" the officer asked.

'The hell'd it look like I was doin'? I was takin' a piss and thinking about how nice it would be if it was your face it was landing on.'

"Sorry officer, I should have gone down to the McDonalds, but it's early, and I couldn't hold it."

He responded with a straight face, but was smiling really big internally about the original answer his thoughts had created.

"You know I could take you in for that right? That's lewd conduct, and destruction of public property, not to mention trespassing. I could really mess up your day right now. You don't want me to do that do you?"

"No sir," Terrance replied, "Not at all sir."

The cop moved forward and grabbed Terrance's hands with his gloved hand and used his feet to spread Terrance's legs apart even more, and then holding his hands tightly together, used his free arm to frisk him down.

"You got anything in your pockets that's gonna hurt me?" He asked, "Anything that's gonna stab or poke me?"

"No sir," Terrance replied

"You ain't got no needles, or syringes in there that I'm gonna stab myself with?"

"No sir."

"What about any drugs? You got anything illegal on you, and be honest, cause we're gonna find it if you do, and if you're lyin' to me I'm gonna take you in."

"No sir."

"You ain't got no crack, or crystal on you?"

"No sir."

"Where's your wallet?" the cop asked.

"Got stolen sir."

"You ain't lyin' to me are you?"

"No sir," Terrance replied, "honest to God."

"Well God ain't here right now, it's you and me, and I don't like it when people lie to me, so I'm gonna ask you *one* more time, you got any I.D. on you?"

"No sir, it was in my wallet."

The cop finished frisking him and stepped back.

"You can go ahead and turn around now," he said. "Slowly." He then threw a glance at the tents lined up along the wall. "What about your friends there, they got anything they shouldn't; any drugs or weapons?"

"I don't know sir," Terrance replied, letting his gaze wander to the other officer that was still standing at the car behind the passenger door with his hand on his gun.

The cop stood there for a moment before turning to his partner and yelling out, "What do you think, should we take him in?"

Emphasizing the control he had over the situation, and the ability he had to make Terrance's life miserable.

"Nah," his partner called back, "Don't want him stickin' up the back seat. We just had this thing washed, and I don't want to go back to the station and have to hose it out again."

"All right," he called out, turning to Terrance. "Guess it's your lucky day, but if I see you pissin' on that wall again, I'm gonna arrest your ass, and you'll be spending the next month and a half at Parker Center. You don't want that now do you?"

"No sir," Terrance replied.

"Alright," the cop said, "then get the hell outta here."

"Thank you sir," Terrance said, lowering his head and walking up the street past the cop car.

"And take a shower," the cop called out from behind him, "you smell like shit."

Terrance held his reply until he was well out of earshot.

"Fuckin' asshole."

He didn't swear much; believed that vulgarity was the language of the ignorant, but he also knew that sometimes, there were no other words that could convey the emotions that a person felt, and on this occasion, those were the only words he could use to satisfy the response he needed to let out.

He made his way to the café, and when he popped his head in the door, Armando was finishing up a transaction with a customer.

He walked in and waited patiently for the person to pay and walk past with their cup before walking up to the counter. He knew that sometimes he had an odor to him; not being able to shower regularly, or even that often for that matter had it's unfortunate side effects, and he knew that it bothered some people, so he was kind enough to try and save people the unpleasantness of having to deal with it, and himself the embarrassment of getting the dirty looks, or people holding their noses and telling him to take a shower.

"Morning Armando," he said with a smile. "You seen Danny around?"

"Nah T-Bone, not this morning, sorry man."

Terrance nodded, and said, "Thanks," then turned to leave.

"Not getting any coffee this morning?" Armando called out just as his back was turned.

He turned and glanced at him quickly. "No, not this morning, I'm runnin kind of light. Old Joe's had a fever the past few days, so my coffee budget has gone to gettin' him soup and some aspirin till he can get workin' again."

"Here man, I got you," Armando said, reaching out to grab a cup and setting it on the counter.

"Nah, I can't man, you know I hate takin' handouts, and besides, you got rent to pay, so you can't afford to be givin' free stuff away to old homeless guys like me. Thanks though"

"Nah T-Bone, it's cool man, I insist," Armando said, holding the cup out with an extended arm.

Terrance paused for a moment, shame starting to build up inside him, and then Armando spoke up with a smile, "Come on man, take the damn cup before I change my mind."

Terrance smiled and moved to the counter to grab the cup, and as he was walking towards the coffee station, stopped and turned around.

"Armando," he began.

"What's up T-Bone?"

"What if I told you that I knew the world was going to end in a week, and that everyone we knew was going to die?"

Armando paused, looking up at Terrance.

"Well, then I'd probably say, I hope we've all done right with our lives, cause we're about to find out what happens after we leave here."

Terrance nodded, pondering if he should tell his friend that he should take his family and try and get as far away as possible, but then realized that there was nowhere he could go to escape, and just kept it inside, turning to make his way to the airpot, and the lever that gave him his morning jumpstart.

Four hours later Terrance had made his quota, and was heading back to the Tropical to see if Danny had stopped by. He knew that he'd swing by for coffee sometimes after school, or to hang out on the patio and play his beat up acoustic guitar, and make up words as he sang along like he always had. He loved to hear him play, it reminded him of his father. His dad had been an amazing blues musician, and he could remember hearing him play all the time when he was growing up, but then he passed away and the music stopped. Now his enjoyment came simply from listening to his walkman and Danny, and with him, it was always a show.

He got back to the café as Armando was leaving.

"Hey T-Bone, you just missed Danny."

"Oh," Terrance replied

"Give me a second, he left some papers for you inside," he said, turning around and heading back into the café.

A moment later the door swung open and Armando stuck his hand out with a stack of papers in it.

"Thanks Armando," Terrance said, taking the stack of papers, and flipping through them quickly.

"You're welcome T-Bone," he said as he walked away. "Oh, and tell crazy old Joe to get better yeah, I don't wanna go findin' out he went and died on us because of some stupid cold, and his ass was too stubborn to go to county."

Terrance smiled. "Will do Armando, thanks."

Armando crossed the street to the small parking lot where his car was, and Terrance decided to take what he called *the back route* to his house, which was Silverlake to Temple, and Temple all the way to Alvarado. It took about twice as long, but was a quieter route, and since he had some reading to do, he figured he could use the mellower course.

* * *

Terrance walked slowly down the street, reading the pages that Danny had left for him at the café. There were articles from NASA on Coronal Mass Ejections and Solar Flares; there were pages of theories, and printouts of scientific journals that talked about x-rays, and cosmic storms that led to power outages and massive fires. There was page after page of events in the past that sounded like microscopic versions of what was about to happen. He toiled over the papers, stopping at the local soccer field to sit and read them thoroughly.

The one that caught his attention the most was a paper that was on something that was referred to as the Carrington Event, which happened in 1859. It went on to say that a solar flare erupted from the sun, and was so large, and so powerful, that it was recorded as having been possible to be seen with the naked eye. The report said that the geomagnetic storm that followed it was so large that it destroyed part of the newly created telegraph network, and had caused fires to break out.

It was exactly like Terrance had watched for the last three days.

He sat there for the next two hours reading page after page, learning about geoeffective storms, and the aurora borealis, or the northern lights as they had become popularly referred to as.

He was convinced that this was what he had been seeing in his visions; it had to be, nothing else could explain it. The next step was figuring out how to survive it.

He knew that it took temperatures of over four hundred and fifty one degrees to ignite dry paper, he'd remembered that from reading the Ray Bradbury novel, Fahrenheit 451, which he'd had to study meticulously for his college literature class many years before. He also knew that it took temperatures much higher than that to cause a living tree to combust, because of the moisture it had inside it, which meant the temperature that was about to hit the earth had to be at least six hundred degrees, which meant that pretty much everything on the face of the planet where the flare hit was going to be instantly burned away. His only hope was going to be getting deep enough underground that the surface would protect him from the blast, and hope that it passed over quickly.

He was now faced with an entirely new set of problems; where was he going to find a place in Los Angeles that was deep enough to shelter him and whoever he could convince to follow him down from the blast, and without money, how was he going to be able to stockpile enough food and water to survive afterwards. He had spent over ten years in the Army in his youth, and had learned how to survive on his own in all manner of environments, but living in a scorched wasteland; that was something they had decided to skip over.

He sat there reading, studying the stack of papers until he had covered everything that Danny had left him. For the next hour he sat in silence, the empty soccer field in front of him, pondering what his next move would be.

He had to find a way underground, and he had to convince as many people as he could to come with him. There was no way to save everyone, but he hoped he could at least save those that were close to him.

He made his way back towards his house, and as he was crossing the intersection where the freeway off-ramp was, he saw Joe sitting on his milk crate, holding his *"I ain't gonna lie, I'm gonna spend it on beer"* sign that he had thought devilishly clever when he wrote it.

He walked up to Joe and asked, "Hey Joe, you got a minute?"

Joe looked at him and said, "I's workin', but 'spose I could take a short break fore' rush hour. Don't won' miss prime time on Friday night, that's money time."

"Let me ask you somethin'," Terrance started. "You were born and raised here weren't you?"

Joe smiled really big, and answered, "I sho was! I was here fore' all these morons, hell, I was here fore' most people that are living here now. Boyle Heights, born and raised."

"Well I have a hypothetical question for you. If the world was going to catch on fire, and the only way to survive was to go underground, where in the city would you go?"

Joe paused for a second, his eyes moving up and to the left as he pondered intently on his options. After a moment he snapped his fingers and exclaimed, "I knows exactly where I go. I go to the ol' tunnels under downtown, that's where I go."

"Old tunnels?" Terrance asked. "What old tunnels?"

Joe smiled and gestured at the extra milk crate he had sitting next to him.

"Grab a sit down," he said.

Terrance sat down and waited for him to start.

"See," Joe began, "There's these ol' tunnels runs under the city downtown. They 'riginally built em' as for the 'riginal subway sysem in the forties, then when the train sysem was redone, they used them fo' running bootleg fo' speakeasies during the probition." He paused for a moment. "I recalls them using em' as fallout shelters when we thought Cuba was gon' send those missiles up our asses, an I remembers for a time in da' eighties, they open em up to folk like us when da' weather'd get nasty."

Terrance looked at him and nodded for a moment. "So you think these tunnels are deep enough down that they could survive a good blast?"

Joe laughed, "Ha! They gots rooms in them tunnels could shelter a hunned people from an atomic bomb. I's pretty sure you could survive a little fire. Beside, most of em's hunneds of feet down from what I can 'member."

Terrance let his head bob again for a moment before speaking up. "One last question before I let you get back to work. You remember how to get down into these tunnels?"

"Well," Joe started, "Far's I can 'member, da' entrance is inside da' ol' Hall of Records buildin down off Temple Street. Lessin' that's where it was when we went down there. Just gotta find the elevator down to em'."

"Thanks Joe," Terrance said, standing up and starting his way to his house.

Revelations

As he was walking away he heard Joe holler at a car that was pulling up to the light., "Help a old bastard get his drink tonight?" He shook his head as he walked up to his tent. "Joe, you old crazy bastard." He said to himself before unzipping the door to his house and crawling inside.

He now had a place to escape to, he just had to hope it was really there, and that Joe wasn't spinning another one of his crazy tales again, because he didn't want to get to downtown, and find out that there was nothing there, and lose his one chance at possibly surviving this thing.

Sunday the 23rd

Terrance woke up shaking, his body covered in a moist layer of perspiration, a light film covering the gooseflesh across his arms and back. He felt his stomach churning, teetering between holding and releasing what little food remained from the night before. No matter how many times he watched it happen, he didn't think he would ever get used to it. Sure, he had seen his fair share of death in Vietnam, but this was different; he was standing there watching it happen, versus seeing it from across fields and through the thick jungles.

He wiped the sweat and tears away with a small handkerchief he had decided to start keeping by the head of the tent, and then sat up and drug his backpack towards him.

He rummaged through, grabbed his t-shirt and socks, and then slipped them on before making his way out and onto his patio.

He decided to walk down to McDonalds to buy a dollar sandwich for breakfast, and be able to use their bathroom. He wanted to wash some of the grime off his face and be able to start the day fresh. Occasionally the people at the shelter downtown would let him use their showers, but he hated going down there; *Nothin' but drug addicts and crazy folk,* he'd tell the other guys. *You practically have to shower with your clothes on, because one time, I was in the shower, and one of those loonies ran off with my shoes and little bit of cash I'd had in my pants.* His list of reasons for keeping the mental separation between guys in a hard spot and the loonies was ever growing the longer he was on the streets.

He went inside and ordered his egg sandwich and asked for a token for the bathroom. The girl hesitated, giving him a look that said how badly she didn't want to, but was obligated to because he had purchased something, thereby making him a customer.

She reached under the counter and set a token in front of him before turning around and going to the bagging station.

He said *thank you*, even though her back was already to him, and then turned to make his way to the bathroom, where he washed his face and neck in the sink; a *bum bath* some folks called it. He finished up and used a handful of paper towels to dry his face, and clean the mess he'd left from inside the sink, and then made his way back outside, where his sandwich was sitting in a paper bag on the counter. He'd come to realize, that most of the time, even if he told them it was going to be to stay, they'd still put it in a bag, kind of a hint to say, get out of here, we don't want you hanging around.

He made his way to one of the tables and sat down, pulling the paper on coronal mass ejections out. He sat there for the next twenty minutes studying the page over and over again while slowly eating his breakfast. When he was finished, he folded the paper back up and stuck it in his pocket, dropped the wasted bag in the trash and made his way to the Tropical.

It was Sunday, so he knew there was a possibility that he'd run into Danny, and he needed to tell him everything he'd learned. They had five days left to gather as much stuff as they could carry, and lead as many people as possible to the tunnels downtown.

When he got to the Tropical, Danny was sitting out front with one of his friends. Terrance walked up and said hello, and then turned to Danny and said, "I really need to talk to you, it's important."

Danny looked up and asked, "Did you get the papers I left you?"

"I did. That's kind of what this is about."

"Look," Terrance started, "I think what's gonna happen is called a coronal mass ejection. It's when a build up of gasses on the sun explode outwards, sending plasma, heat and radiation hurling through space at millions of miles an hour." He paused digging the folded paper out of his pocket. "It says here that it's happened before, and has caused massive power outages, and in a few cases, fires. I think this is what's gonna happen, only much, *much* bigger. And I know when it's gonna hit us."

Danny's friend looked at him and raised his eyebrows for a second, a small grin of amusement creeping onto his face. He stood up and looked at Danny. "I'm gonna go ahead and take off now, hit me up later yeah?" he said, "And if you can get me some of whatever this guys on, that'd be awesome." He turned and started walking up the street.

"Later Dom," he shouted, turning back to Terrance and apologizing.

"Sorry man."

"Look. Danny. This thing's gonna happen on the twenty-eighth. That's *six days* from now."

Danny took a deep breath and asked, "You want a cup of coffee? I got a couple bucks on me."

Terrance nodded, "That'd be nice, thank you Danny."

He got up and made his way inside, leaving Terrance to replay the burning palm trees, and young woman over in his head for a moment before pulling his gaze back to the table in front of him.

A moment later Danny came walking back outside with two cups of coffee, setting one in front of Terrance and saying, "Touch of sugar right, little cream to cool it off?"

Terrance smiled. "You're a good kid Danny."

After a moment Danny looked up at Terrance and said, "Look T-Bone, I don't exactly know what to think of all this. I mean, you gotta look at it from my perspective. Two days ago you walked up to me, and told me you were having, crazy, *psychic visions* of the end of the world, and now you're telling me that it's gonna happen in six days." He shrugged. "What am I supposed to think, I mean, come on dude, it sounds fuckin' nuts."

"Language." Terrance responded, raising an eyebrow above the papers he was scanning.

"Sorry. It sounds crazy."

"Look, I know it does, but I'm telling you the truth. I *know* this is going to happen. These aren't just dreams, they're more than that. They're *real*."

Danny took another deep breath, letting his gaze fall to the large mural on the side of the pharmacy across the street.

"So what are we supposed to do then?" He asked. "You say the worlds coming to an end, there's not exactly much we can do right? So what's the point of worrying about it, shouldn't we be out there trying to get fu... messed up, and getting laid and stuff; enjoying our last days on earth?"

Terrance shook his head. "Actually, I think I have an idea." He paused, taking a sip of his coffee. "If the blast is going to hit the surface of the planet, then that means that the heat will stay on top, so anything beneath the surface will be fine, I asked around, and apparently, there's some old tunnels in downtown that used to be used in the fifties for evacuation drills, running illegal liquor and other things like that. As it would, I've heard that one of these tunnels has a rather large fallout shelter in it, and if I'm correct, it should be deep enough to not be affected by the blast on the surface." He paused. "Heat dissipation through soil and all that."

Danny smiled, pointing his finger at Terrance and bobbing it up and down. "I've heard of those tunnels. People still use em' to get from building to building when it's raining pretty bad. I think people still go jogging and stuff in em too."

"Yeah," Terrance said, "those are the ones. All we need to do is stock up enough stuff to last a few days, and on the twenty-seventh, we'll make our way down there with as many people as we can, and wait for the blast to finish. Then we can go back up, and try and start over."

Danny stared at him for a moment, a puzzled look slowly working its way across his features. "And just how do you expect to get people to listen to an old homeless guy and some kid to A; believe this crazy story, and B; to actually follow us down there?" He paused, his brows knitting together for a moment. "Actually, now that you mention it, the idea's kinda freakin me out too."

"Look, I'm being serious Danny. This is the only way we're gonna survive this."

"Alright, alright." Danny said. "I'll see what I can rummage up from around the house. My dad's one of those survivalist, *zombie apocalypse* type guys, so I think I can get a good amount of stuff, just as long as he doesn't notice."

"You're not gonna tell your folks?" Terrance asked.

Danny shook his head. "What am I supposed to tell them, that this old homeless guy I'm friends with is saying that the world's about to end because we're gonna get hit by some massive solar eruption from the sun, and I have to take a bunch of the family survival gear, and go break into the abandoned tunnels in downtown for a couple days?" He paused. "Somehow I don't see that conversation going over so well."

Terrance nodded. "I guess you're right."

"I know I'm right. Trust me, and I know my dad. The second I mention that to him, he'll have me locked in my room for the next week."

Terrance stayed quiet.

"So what do we need then?" Danny asked.

"Well," Terrance started, "We'll need plenty of water, some canned food, couple flashlights, matches, toilet paper, and socks."

Danny looked at him puzzled. "Socks?"

"Yeah," Terrance said, "if the world comes to an end, you're gonna be awful grateful to have a few pairs of socks on you. Trust me, you'd be surprised how quick your feet can go to hell, and something tells me we're gonna be doing a lot of walking after this is over, so..."

"Ok," Danny said with a chuckle, "socks it is." He took another sip of his coffee, then asked Terrance, "Who else are you gonna tell?"

Terrance looked at him and said, "As many as I can Danny, as many as will listen."

Danny's brow furled together and he looked around him. "None of these people give a shit about you, why even bother. It's not like they'd go out of their way to tell you the world was coming to an end. Fuck em."

"Language!" Terrance said, reprimanding Danny again for his use of vulgarity.

Danny sighed. "But seriously, why?"

Terrance looked at him and smiled. "You see, that's just what the problem is with the world, no one's willing to help someone else, less'n their getting helped themselves." He paused shaking his head, knowing how difficult it must be for a boy as young, and inexperienced as Danny was to understand what he was trying to say. "The worlds never going to change, unless everyone decides to change it, so all we can do, is change ourselves, and hope that everyone else jumps on board." He paused, taking a sip of his coffee. "Believe it or not Danny, there's more good people in this world than there are bad, it's just the bad ones that get all the attention, so the world only focuses on them. I have hope for this world, so if there's anything I can do to help it, regardless of how I've been treated, or the hands I've been dealt, then I will." He paused again. "I'm just not sure how now."

"Well," Danny said, "Whatever it is, you better think of it quick."

"You ain't got anybody you'd wanna bring with us do you?" Terrance asked.

Danny thought for a moment. "Well I guess there's one guy I might tell, his name's Donny. He lives up the hill few streets from me, cool dude, little older. I think he might be down, and he has a little red car that we could use to transport our stuff to downtown for the night. I'll talk to him."

Terrance nodded. "Well, I better be gettin' off to work, gonna need to make some extra cash if I wanna pick up enough stuff for us."

"All right man," Danny said with a smile." Ill catch you tomorrow."

* * *

Terrance walked down the street to his work spot. He didn't know if Danny believed him or not, he was guessing that he didn't, but it didn't matter, he knew the truth; he had to gather as much stuff as he could, and get as many people as he could to follow him into the tunnels before the 28th, and time was quickly running out.

He made it to his work spot, and after four hours had made a good thirty dollars; enough for a small dinner and a bottle of water. He figured he'd stash the rest away. *'No sense building up a stockpile, and then coming home to find it's all gone.'*

He hit the Burger King on the corner, and then shot down Alvarado to his house. When he got there, Jimmy was stepping out of his door, and turned to him. "T-Bone! We were just about to play some cards up top, you down homie?"

"Nah man, think I'll pass tonight, but you fellas have fun alright."

"Word homes!" Jimmy responded, turning to quickly make his way up the side embankment with a can of Steel Reserve in his hand.

Terrance climbed into his house and settled in to attempt to formulate a plan. He wanted to help as many people as possible, and only had a few days to do it. It would take some serious thinking to let everyone know, but he had to.

He lay down. And stared at the picture of his family, thinking about all the possible ways for him to tell the world that they only had a week left to live, and that they had to make their way underground. His thoughts were swirling as he fell asleep, and it wasn't until he felt the hot, midday sun that he realized he was once again, *dreaming*.

* * *

Terrance looked around and saw a landscape he'd never seen before. It was just becoming nightfall, and he was in another large city, but he'd never been to this one. Everywhere he looked there was water, and it became obvious that it was a seaside metropolis.

He looked to his left and saw a bridge spanning across a bay, and when he shifted his gaze to the right, saw a large white structure sticking up like contrasting waves in the ocean. He recognized the building, and after a few moments it hit him, *'It's the Sydney Opera House. I'm in Australia."*

He began to walk towards the landmark when he realized that this had to be more than just a dream. He had never been to Australia before, so there was no way his mind could recreate something so vividly, that it had never seen before.

Revelations

He began walking down the street, waiting for the heat and the brightness, but it stayed still. At the point in which his other visions the sky would be on fire, and the landscape would be burning, the people were still walking around, unphased. Then he saw someone look at their phone and scream. It was only moments later that the same reaction began all around him; people looking at their phones, and laptops and running away, leaving their computers, and food where it was sitting. It made no sense. Where was the fire... the burning?

He stayed there for quite some time, watching the world around him erupt into a panic, and then his eyes moved to the horizon.

Off in the distance he could see a dark mass moving towards them, like a thundercloud moving very fast, or the smoke that plumes from an erupting volcano.

There was no heat, just darkness.

Donald Morrison

The smell approached first; burnt earth and acrid fumes wafting past before the shroud of darkness spread itself across the sky with a large gust of hot wind.

He stood there for a while as the sky became blackened out, and realized, *'There's no fire. Australia isn't burning..."*

Monday the 24th

Terrance woke up and tossed around a bit uneasily. How he was supposed to tell the world that it was about to end in a fiery inferno was running his brain in circles. He heard a small cough come from Joe's house and decided he should start with his friends first.

He slowly got dressed, and before leaning forward to unzip his house called out, "Hey Joe, you awake in there?"

"Am now," a sleepy reply answered back.

"Look," Terrance started, "I'm gonna hit the restaurant on the corner and grab some breakfast for you and the guys, I need you to get everyone up. I have something important I need to talk to ya'll about, alright?"

"You buyin' breakfast T-Bone?" Joe responded.

"Yes Joe... I'm buying breakfast."

"I'll get the fellas up," Joe said, starting to sound a little more motivated.

113

Terrance unzipped his door and made his way down the street. It was still early, and the city was just starting to get its early bustle.

He walked into the McDonalds, ordered eight egg sandwiches, and used the bathroom, giving his hands and face a quick wash.

He came back out, grabbed his warm bag of food, and made his way back to the camp.

As he walked up he saw Joe and Jimmy standing on the patio, and heard Mad Dog grumbling something or another. He walked up and looked at Joe with a smile and said, "Well, it looks like I'll just have me a couple extra egg and sausage sandwiches this morning then."

"You better hurry up homie," Jimmy said, his words aimed at Mad Dog's tent, a smile spread across his face. "I might just have to tax one too."

"I'm coming, don't get your lacies all in a bunch," Mad Dog said from inside. A minute later he was stepping out onto the concrete, rubbing the sleep from his eyes. "This better be important, I was having a good dream."

They made their way up to the back porch on the hill and sat down around the table. Terrance divvied out the breakfast sandwiches and began telling the guys about his dreams. He told them about Sunset, and Santa Monica, and San Francisco and Australia; about the fire and death that was going to occur. They all sat there eating quietly while T-Bone spun his tale of impending apocalypse, and when he was finished, he looked around the table and said, "So we need to figure out how to get as much stuff as possible to the Hall of Records by the 27th, that way we can be underground by the time this solar flare thing hits."

Joe scratched his head for a moment and glanced to the others.

"So lets just say we manage to get a bunch of stuff put together," Mad Dog began, "How you suggestin' we supposed to get it down into them tunnels? Somethin' tells me they ain't gon' be to keen on a group of homeless guys moving they shit in, and I highly doubt their gon' believe yo' end a da world shit."

"I'm still workin' on that part," Terrance replied.

"You know," Jimmy said, his eyes squinting slightly, "I might just have us an idea."

All eyes shot to him.

"Lay it on us," Terrance said, intrigue laced through his words.

"Well I was just thinkin'. I use to have a lot a homies that were in crews you know. They'd go out and do those big murals you'd see, and late night missions hittin' up freeway signs and shit. Well, what they'd do to keep the pigs from thinkin they was tagging, was they'd wear those bright orange city vests, and white helmets." He paused smiling in reminiscence. "They'd even go as far as to set up the lights so that shit'd look legit. For real. Hide in plain sight type shit you know."

Terrance nodded. "You don't happen to still know any of those guys do you?" he asked.

"I ain't spoke to them in a minute," he responded, "but I still know where they kick it. I'm pretty sure for a twelve pack they'd let us borrow their stuff, we just gotta come up with a good story why, cause I don't think these vatos are gonna be down for this end of the world shit."

"Alright," Terrance said, "I'll leave that up to you then.

Jimmy nodded. "For sure homie, I got you."

"I got somethin' for us," Mad Dog said.

Terrance nodded to him.

"Down the way, there's this water bottle delivery guy, lazy mufukka too. He stops at St. Vincent to deliver to the offices. Dude never locks his shit up, ever. I used to go get me a bottle every now and the, just cause it was so easy. I mean damn, dude practically givin the shit away." He smiled at Terrance. "Wouldn't be too hard to grab three or four of those jugs, slap em on a dolly and make my way back here. Hell, nobody in that neighborhood gives two shits about anything anyways. Half the time they don't even report gunshots."

"That's good Mad Dog, that's real good," Terrance replied, starting to feel a touch of hope. "What about you Joe, you got anything for us?"

"Well." Joe said with a grin. "You gon' need yo'self a good distracshun, and ain't nobody better than me fo dat'!"

He was right too. Guitar Joe had no sense of morals, no shame, and no sense of embarrassment. One time he bit into a dead squirrel, just to get at the "rich white folk" that were staring at him. *Teach them sons a bitches to stare at ol' Guitar Joe.*

Terrance nodded. "That's good Joe."

He didn't bother trying to formulate a plan with him, he knew Joe would already forget about it by the time they stood up from the table, he was just bein' polite, and involving him in the conversation.

"All right then," Terrance said. "Now I just gotta figure out how to tell as many people as possible that they gotta either get underground, or had to Australia before the 28th."

"You could draw yourself up a sign like, the world's coming to an end, get underground, or something like that," Mad Dog said.

"Yeah, I was kinda thinkin' about that," Terrance replied. "Think I'm also going to just try and tell as many people as I can also, might have a little better luck with it that way."

"You know most people ain't gonna listen, right?" Jimmy said. "They only look at us a crazy homeless fools and gangsters. They think we all crackheads and shit."

"I know Jimmy, but I have to try. If I don't, then what was the point of me having these visions? It feels like I was chosen for a reason, and somethin' tells me, it wasn't just to save myself."

"Just sayin' homie, don't expectin' too much eh."

"I know Jimmy," Terrance said. "Well look fellas, I'd love to sit here all day and get old with you guys, but I gotta planet to go try and save, so, I'll catch ya'll later."

"Alright then," Mad Dog said, followed by a head nod and, "Orelay homes," From Jimmy. Joe just stuck his hand up and nodded.

* * *

Terrance made his way down Sunset. The first person he needed to tell was Armando. He'd always been someone he considered a friend, and he had a family. He had always taken care of Terrance, now it was his turn to return the favor; it was just getting him to believe him that was going to be the hard part.

As he approached the Tropical he saw Armando behind the counter. He walked in and asked him, "Armando, I have something *really important* I need to talk to you about, you gonna have a minute today?"

Armando looked at him and smiled. "Yeah, I think I do, what's up man?"

"We should probably talk when you're not working. It's kind of a life and death conversation."

Armando's face dropped. "You're not dyin' are you? Is it cancer man? *Fuck* I hate cancer."

"No, no, I'm not dying. I just really need to talk to you." Terrance said in a very serious tone.

"Damnit T-Bone, you scared the shit out of me homie." He took a deep breath and shook his head. "Come back at five, I'll be getting off then alright?"

"Sure thing Armando, thanks."

As he was turning to leave he paused, and then turned around. "Hey Armando, you ain't got a marker I could get do you?"

"Yeah, I think I got somethin' around here," he said, digging around under the register. "Here ya go man."

"Thanks," Terrance said, grabbing the marker and putting it in his pocket.

"No worries," Armando said, "Just make sure not to lose it yeah."

"You got it," Terrance replied, already making his way quickly outside.

He made his way back up towards his work spot; he knew he'd be able to find a box large enough to spread his message with behind the Rite Aid.

When he got there, he broke one of the large cardboard boxes open, ripped the edges off of the largest piece, and sat down to write his message.

He sat there with the black marker in his hand for quite some time, trying to figure out what he was going to write, without sounding like a crazy person. He was beginning to realize how difficult it was going to be.

When he finished writing his message in bold black lettering, he set it down and stepped back to make sure people would be able to read it as they came towards him. It read, "Solar flare to hit earth on Friday, the 28th. Get underground, or to a fallout shelter for safety. Please listen."

He decided to leave out the Australia part, cause most people wouldn't be able to go there anyways, but getting underground, there were fallout shelters throughout the city.

He picked his sign up and made his way to his work spot, where he tied it up to the crosswalk sign with a shoelace, and went to work.

Every time he'd get handed change, he'd tell them to read the sign, that it was important. Of the five hours he was there, only one person asked him where he'd heard that, and when he told him in the abridged, between lights version that he was having visions of it, the guy laughed and rolled his window up.

He could feel that it was pointless, but he had to keep trying, there was nothing else he could do.

The sun was starting to set, so he checked his watch. 4:40.

He packed his stuff up and made his way to the Tropical. When he got there, Armando was locking up.

He grabbed a seat on the curb and told him everything. He had said it enough times now that it was almost beginning to sound rehearsed.

Armando sat and listened to him, nodding his head, and saying, "OK," every now and then, and when he finished up, he said, "So we're gonna try and make it down to the tunnels. You need to get your family and meet us there."

Armando stayed quiet for a moment, and then spoke in a soft, friendly tone. "Look T-Bone," he began, trying hard to not come off as patronizing, "I've known you for a long time, and I know you're not like all these other crazy ass homeless fools that run around, covered in piss and talking to themselves; but I can't just pack up my family, and follow you and Danny to some tunnels under the city because you've been having some really bad dreams man. It just doesn't work that way you know." He paused. "I got a wife and two kids that depend on me man. I just.... I don't know what to tell you man..."

"I know," Terrance said, determination in his voice. "That's why I'm telling you this. I'm not lying, or making this up. This is *real*, and it's gonna happen in less than a week. We got five days man. Then this," he said, spreading his arms out and looking at the world around him, "all of this, is gone. Everything we know is going to be burnt. Scorched..."

Armando took another deep breath. "I wanna believe you T-Bone, I really do," he said sadly, "but I mean," he paused again. "How can I. How am I supposed to believe this enough to pack up my family and leave, just because you tell me I have to. I've had people tell me to buy a lottery ticket before, but I'm still here, workin' at this café ya know. You see what I'm sayin' man?"

"Please Armando. Please. You have to believe me."

Armando stayed quiet for a moment, and then let his gaze fall to the ground between his feet. "I'm sorry man."

Terrance nodded.

"Look, uh, I gotta get goin man, my wife's off work at six and I gotta pick her up, but um, you take care of yourself yeah. I worry about you."

Terrance nodded. "I know Armando. And if you change your mind, you know where we're heading."

Armando nodded, and then stood up, said, "Take it easy man," and then walked across the street to his car.

Terrance sat there for a while, even after Armando had driven off.

'Why won't anyone believe me?' he thought to himself, before shaking his head slowly and bringing himself to his feet. He started his way back up sunset, and as he was getting to Alvarado, decided to take a walk around the lake before heading home.

Revelations

As he approached the park, there were two police cars, and they were arresting a homeless couple that had been hanging out near the boathouse. He thought it best if he kept walking, and just made his loop around the park without actually going in.

He stopped at the tennis courts, and watched a couple matches before making his way up Temple to his house, where he crawled in and settled down for the night. He pondered taking another swig off the rum bottle, and then thought better of it, putting it back in his backpack, and laying down to begin the long process of falling asleep to the symphony of city noise around him.

When he opened his eyes, it wasn't like the visions he'd had before. There was no trees, or birds in the sky; no people going about their day, ignorant of the oncoming destruction.

He was standing in the parking lot of the Griffith Observatory; or what used to be the observatory.

Everything was burnt. There were no trees left, no plant life, nothing. He scanned the parking lot, and there were dozens of burnt out cars; windows and tires gone; melted onto the ground below, and they all had the same, rust colored coating where the paint had boiled off.

He saw countless skeletons lying about, some huddled together, some sprawled in the parking lot, arms stretched out, reaching for some unseen object. It reminded him of the National Geographic images of Pompeii that he'd seen in his cultural studies class in college, but without the layer of ash covering everything.

He started to make his way to the observatory, noticing that it was unusually dark outside, like when a solar eclipse would happen, and it would look overcast, but still feel like midday.

He walked around the edge of the observatory and stopped, his heart sinking, and jaw slightly opening at the same time.

Below him, the entire Los Angeles valley was burnt. He slowly panned his head, and saw that all the way from Pasadena to the beach in Venice was a blackened, scorched wasteland.

Smoke was rising in the air, and he could see where gas mains had ruptured; fire shooting towards the sky in steady streams.

He stood there staring at the carbonized earth, realizing that millions of people had been wiped out of existence, burnt to nothing more than skeletal remains in a matter of seconds.

Sadness began to tear at him, and he felt hopelessness flowing through his veins. Millions had died, and there was nothing he could do to save them.

"Why!?" he screamed. "Why are you doing this to me? Why are you showing me this!? What do you want from me?"

Donald Morrison

He fell to his knees, staring at the blackened city below and sobbed. He sobbed for the death of everyone he couldn't save, he sobbed for the families that had been erased, for the friends and neighbors that had died without a chance, for his friends, and the family he'd never see again.

He sat there in a crumpled heap, his legs folded beneath him and sobbed, as he stared out into a valley of death, the intense heat swirling angrily around him.

Tuesday the 25ᵗʰ

Terrance woke up, and the first words that entered his mind were, *'Four days.'*

He stared at the ceiling of his house for a moment before throwing his clothes on and making his way outside.

Traffic was already flowing, and he could tell by the amount of cars, and the sound of the freeway above that he'd slept later than usual; the sounds of the city told him that without having to glance at his watch.

He rolled his head in a circle, loosening up his neck and giving his arms a long, wide stretch before making his way up the street to his spot. He wanted to get work out of the way early so he could use the rest of the day to try and tell as many people as possible, and start putting preparations together.

He made his way to his intersection and tied his cardboard warning up for the passerby's to see, and went to work, collecting what he needed to purchase supplies for after the stores were gone.

Three hours went by like nothing, and when he looked at his watch it was already two o'clock. He gave his pocket a quick lift from the bottom, and guessed at about thirteen bucks in change, and tallied with the mental note of seventeen dollars in bills, had enough to get himself a cheap dinner, and some supplies from the surplus store in Hollywood.

He hung out for another hour, just to fluff his budget a bit, then wrapped his sign up and made his way back down Sunset where he caught the number 4 to Santa Monica and Vine.

When he stepped off the bus he made his way into the surplus store, and approached the woman at the counter. "Excuse me Miss, where could I find your water purification tablets and MRE's?"

She looked him up and down quickly, and then said, "Gonna be back there, behind the boots."

He nodded, saying, "Thank you kindly," and then made his way to the back.

When he got to the back section there was box after box, loaded with different kinds of MRE's, and a small shelf that had waterproof matches, and water purification tablets and devices.

He did some quick calculations and grabbed three bottles of tablets, enough to last him a couple months if he worked it right, and a handful of rations, two weeks if he spread it out.

He walked back to the front, and put his collection on the counter. The woman gave him a puzzled look and smiled. "Preparing for the apocalypse?"

He exhaled a single chuckle at the irony of her remark and said, "Somethin' like that."

She rang him up and said, "That'll be twenty-eight dollars and fifty-three cents."

He handed her the bills first, and then apologized about the change, counting it out for her so she didn't have to go through the trouble.

She waited patiently, and then placed his things in a bag. "Have a nice day," she said, her eyes already moving to a younger man who had walked in.

He replied, "You do the same," and then made his way back outside.

As he walked towards the bus stop it hit him that he hadn't walked from Hollywood back to his house in a really long time, and it was turning out to be a really nice afternoon for a stroll. *'Might not get the chance to do this one again..,"* he thought to himself, changing his course of direction, dropping down Vine to Beverly, and cutting across.

He strolled for the better part of an hour, leisurely taking his time, admiring the flowers that grew, and the nice houses that lined Beverly between Rossmore and Western. He thought quietly to himself, *'I really should have done this a lot more,'* as the thought of the city lying in ashes passed like a bullet through his mind.

As he came to the train station on Beverly and Vermont, he wondered if the tunnels would be deep enough to protect whoever was riding the trains from the cataclysmic blast that would occur above their unknowing heads. He knew the tunnels were deep, but didn't know if they'd be deep enough to keep the trains from becoming superheated compartments in a tunnel of fire.

He continued to walk on, enjoying the air as the sun began to set behind him, spreading its crimson hue across the sky, and he looked up to see the moon large and contrasting against the fading blue backdrop.

It was another twenty minutes before he was back home, and when he arrived, Joe was still sitting on his milk crate, an almost empty forty of King Cobra at his feet, his big toothless grin causing passerby's to roll their windows up to avoid an awkward interaction on their way to wherever it was they were going.

"Whatcha got there T-Bone?" Joe called out as he was crossing the street towards him.

"Got myself some provisions, starting to stock up for our trip," he answered, glancing at the yellow bag in his hand.

"Trip?" Joe asked. "Where we goin?"

Terrance smiled. "I'll tell ya in three days Joe, just make sure you're around yeah."

"Ha!" Joe belted, "Just where the *hell* you think I'ma off to?"

Terrance chuckled as he walked past. "Hey Joe, you seen Jimmy?"

"Nah," Joe responded, not looking back, "Left a little while ago. Said something about getting a vest or somethin. Guessn' he gots himself a date or somthin"

"Alright Joe," Terrance said, making his way towards his house.

* * *

It was a few hours later when he heard a call come from outside, and a Jimmy's voice came though the tent.

"T-Bone, you in there homes?"

"Yeah," Terrance said, leaning forward to throw his shirt on, "be out in a second."

"Alright homie, I got some news for you."

"Comin'," Terrance said, leaning forward to unzip his door.

"What's up Jimmy?" he asked, turning around to zip his tent up.

"Look man," Jimmy began, looking around in his usual paranoid fashion, "So I talked to the homies yeah."

"Ok?" Terrance asked during a dramatic pause. "And..?"

"Well the good new is, they have the vests and helmets."

Terrance waited for a moment, and then slightly puzzled, asked, "And.... The bad news?"

"Well," Jimmy continued, looking around again, "Those fools want cash homes. And like the kind we ain't got."

Terrance sighed, bringing his hand up to rub his forehead. "How much are we talking?"

"They want a hundred bucks homie."

"A hundred dollars," Terrance said, starting to feel at a loss. "And how the hell they expect four homeless guys to come up with that kind of money?"

"They're from the hood homie, they give a shit *where* we get the money from, but they ain't giving us what we want till they get it."

"Damn," Terrance said. "Well, it looks like we've gotta come up with something else then."

Jimmy paused for a moment, staring at Terrance, as if trying to see what was in his soul through his eyes. "I gotta ask you this, and I need you to be *real* honest with me homie. You're not fuckin' around when it comes to this whole end of the world thing are you, like, you *know* this shit's gonna happen right?"

Terrance looked at him in the eyes. "No Jimmy, I'm not, this is real."

Jimmy bit his lower lip and bobbed his head. "Alright homes, I hope so." He paused. "Look, don't worry about the money alright, I gotta figure some things out, but I got you fool. Don't worry eh."

Terrance nodded. He knew he probably wouldn't approve of whatever means Jimmy would use to acquire the cash they needed, so he decided it was better not to ask how he was gonna get it, he just nodded and said, "Thanks Jimmy."

"No worries homie, I got this," he said, turning to make his way down the street towards Silver Lake.

Terrance watched him walk away, and then when he was about a block down, he turned and made his way back inside his house, pulling out a Stephen King book he had found at the Goodwill, and laying in his bed to get some reading in before he went to sleep.

Two hours passed, and when he realized he was dozing off in the middle of a paragraph, he folded the corner of the page he was on, and put Danny Torrance and The Overlook Hotel in his backpack and lay down to let sleep take control.

Revelations

Wednesday the 26th

When Terrance woke up, his arms were up, shielding his face from the flames and heat that had just moments ago wrapping itself around him. The vision of Central Park engulfed in a falling inferno with the Statue of Liberty standing sadly in the distance was etched into his sight.

He pushed back the screams, and sounds of animals in their death throws, locked in searing cages as the zoo went up in flames.

He took a large shuddered breath and forced himself into a seated position, pulling his saturated t-shirt off and tossing it to the foot of the tent.

He felt nauseous, and his head was swimming in a dizzy blur. He leaned forward and no sooner unzipped his front door, than his stomach lurched and he emptied the small contents onto the porch in front of him.

When he was done retching he fell back into his tent, and sat there for a

Revelations

Wednesday the 26th

When Terrance woke up, his arms were up, shielding his face from the flames and heat that had just moments ago wrapping itself around him. The vision of Central Park engulfed in a falling inferno with the Statue of Liberty standing sadly in the distance was etched into his sight.

He pushed back the screams, and sounds of animals in their death throws, locked in searing cages as the zoo went up in flames.

He took a large shuddered breath and forced himself into a seated position, pulling his saturated t-shirt off and tossing it to the foot of the tent.

He felt nauseous, and his head was swimming in a dizzy blur. He leaned forward and no sooner unzipped his front door, than his stomach lurched and he emptied the small contents onto the porch in front of him.

When he was done retching he fell back into his tent, and sat there for a

Revelations

Wednesday the 26th

When Terrance woke up, his arms were up, shielding his face from the flames and heat that had just moments ago wrapping itself around him. The vision of Central Park engulfed in a falling inferno with the Statue of Liberty standing sadly in the distance was etched into his sight.

He pushed back the screams, and sounds of animals in their death throws, locked in searing cages as the zoo went up in flames.

He took a large shuddered breath and forced himself into a seated position, pulling his saturated t-shirt off and tossing it to the foot of the tent.

He felt nauseous, and his head was swimming in a dizzy blur. He leaned forward and no sooner unzipped his front door, than his stomach lurched and he emptied the small contents onto the porch in front of him.

When he was done retching he fell back into his tent, and sat there for a

141

moment before reaching next to his bag for a bottle of water, and draining it in a quick succession of gulps.

He tossed the empty bottle behind him and sat there staring at the grey concrete wall across from him on the other side of the street.

He watched blankly as car after car went past, his eyes not moving from the empty space they were fixated on.

Eventually he lifted the brick that was his wrist, and checked the time; 7:46 A.M.

He rubbed his face, and blew the remaining chunks out of his nose before digging in his bag, and grabbing socks and his last clean shirt.

When he had gotten dressed, he took a mouthful of generic mouthwash and zipped up his house, swishing for a moment, and then spitting it into the street, and making his way towards the park.

He decided that since it was still to early to go to Tropical to see if Danny had shown up, and that nobody gave out cash this early, so going to work would be pointless, that he'd take himself a stroll around the lake.

When he got there, the birds had just started making their way out for their morning baths, and the ducks out for breakfast.

He started making his way around the lake when he began to hear a ringing in his ears. It started slow, but was gradually increasing in intensity with every step he took. The moment he though his eardrums were going to explode, everything went silent, and the scene before him changed.

The boathouse had become a fire-ravaged husk, reduced to a burned rubble; the only thing still standing, the brick structure that had held the base up. The bottom of the lake was bone dry, and there were no birds to be seen. The boats were nothing more than a multicolored plastic coating along the side of the dried cement basin, and the ground was grey with ash where the vibrant grass had been just moments ago.

He scanned the park and saw countless skeletons along the cement path that circled the lake, charred husks of the people that had been jogging around it, or chatting with their friends. He saw the incinerated remains of a stroller, with two skeletons crumpled at its base, a family out for a morning stroll, taken without any notice.

He walked through the surreal landscape, the deafening silence adding to the eerie visage. As he took it all in, he began to hear the ringing in his ears again, followed by the type of pressure he felt when being on a 747 as it took to the sky. A moment later everything flashed back to normal, and he was surrounded by the sounds of Echo Park waking up; ducks quaking in the lake, and the occasional bird chirping from the trees; the distant sound of traffic beginning to invade the quiet.

He stood there trembling, his brain feeling like he had just stuck a fork in a light socket, as he tried to compose himself.

"What is happening to me?" he whispered to the chorus of birds that were gathering.

He slowly started to walk again, with every step afraid that the world around him would once again contort into the twisted vision that he had just walked through.

He continued on, slowly making his way around the lake to the benches at the back. His mind was reeling with the fact that he no longer had to be sleeping to receive these visions of destruction. He strolled in the early morning light as the city unfolded its sleepy arm from around him, arms that would soon be charred and black, left nothing more than ashen remains.

He sat on the bench for quite a while, waiting till the sun was well into the sky before standing up and making his way back up to Sunset, and down to his morning cup of coffee.

When he arrived at the Tropical, Lucy was inside. For an instant he was almost glad, he didn't want to deal with the embarrassing awkward exchange with Armando.

He opened the door and stepped in. "Morning Lucy," he said, walking up to the counter. "How are you doing on this fine day?"

"Hey T-Bone," she answered with a smile, "I'm doing good, thanks." She paused, setting a stack of napkins on the counter. "The usual?" she asked.

"Yeah," he replied, "but hold the muffin this morning. Gotta watch my figure," he said with a smile.

He didn't want to try and explain that he had to save his money to buy supplies for the end of the world. Not a conversation he was trying to have this early, especially with the image of it still fresh in his mind.

Lucy chuckled and said, "Oh, ok," with a playful tone of sarcasm layered behind it. "Aren't we all?"

He grinned and slid his four dollars across the counter, to which she smiled softly, took two and pushed the rest back towards him.

He smiled. "Thanks Lucy," he said, dropping one of them in the empty tip jar. "Lets get you started."

"Thank you T-Bone," she said with the smile that always warmed his heart.

He made his way to the coffee station to fill his cup.

"You have a good one you hear," he said, turning to make his way back outside.

"You too T-Bone," she said as the door closed behind him.

He walked to one of the tables and sat down. He hoped that Danny would stop by before heading to school, and just as the thought was leaving his mind he heard the sound of skateboard wheels clacking up the sidewalk.

He turned to see Danny riding down Sunset towards him, and said, "Speak of the devil."

Donald Morrison

"Sup T-Bone?" he called as he rode across the intersection to the café.

"Hey Danny," he said, pounding fists with him when he walked up.

"Let me grab my coffee," he said, "got some good news for you."

"Cool," Terrance said, sitting back down and letting his gaze wander to a young hip couple making their way down the street.

'Why is it that guys wanna dress like their girlfriends these days? What the hell is wrong with these kids? How the hell you pull your pants up when they that skinny, pliers?'

He stared as the couple in their matching Ray-Bans walked past, and as soon as they were out of sight Danny stepped out of the café and grabbed a seat next to him.

"So," he started, "my pops thinks I'm gonna be spending the night at Ian's house Friday night, so just in case nothing happens, at least I won't get grounded. And I managed to get some stuff out of the "prep shed". I got a couple bottles of those

148

purification tablets, ten boxes of waterproof matches, some flints, an assload of socks, and a couple of those heat blankets just in case; the silver ones that protect you from fire. I'm also gonna load up with a bunch of those ready to eat packaged meals before I go too, that way, if this shit does go down, at least we can eat for a couple weeks."

Terrance nodded with a big smile on his face. "Thatta boy. Good work my man, put her here." He stuck out his fist again for Danny to pound.

"What about that friend of yours, Donny I think you said his name was?"

"Well, if he can get his grandma's car, then he's down. I invited my girlfriend to come along, I hope you don't mind."

Terrance realized that the seriousness of everything had yet to set in with him, and that he was still just viewing this as a little "adventure getaway", not knowing what was really going to happen. There was no way for him to; he hadn't seen what Terrance had.

"That's just fine," Terrance said with a smile. "The more the merrier."

"Awesome!" Danny said. "So what's the plan then? How we gonna get the stuff downtown if Donny falls through?"

"Well," Terrance said, making it up as he spoke, "I was thinking we could just go with the old *homeless train*." He paused, letting a smile cross his face as he realized that it actually might be a good idea. "See, we just get three or four carts and we strap em together with whatever we can, and we make kind of a train out of em'. One person pushes from behind, one pulls in front, and the others guide it, making sure it don't fall over, or get stuck in any cracks. Might take us a while to get there, but if all goes well, we have a way in."

"Really?" Danny asked. "How do you figure?"

"Well," Terrance replied. "That one we're just gonna have to wait and see."

"Well," Danny said with a grin. "I for one can't wait. This is gonna be awesome!"

Terrance nodded, mustering every ounce of charade's he had inside him to pull a smile to his mouth. "It's definitely gonna be *somethin'*..."

"Well, I gotta be getting' off to school, late already, as usual, but where are we supposed to meet at, and when?"

Terrance thought about the visions, and tried quickly to place where the sun was in the sky. When it happened in L.A. he remembered putting his arm almost directly over his head, making it around mid-day.

"Go ahead and meet me where I stay at under the 101 overpass on Alvarado, right before you get to Temple. Better get there early too, I'm thinking right around the time the sun comes up, say seven."

"Awesome!" Danny said, turning to leave.

"Danny!" Terrance said, just as he'd dropped his skateboard to the ground.

"What's up?" he asked quickly as he turned around.

"You can't be late. Not this time, it's more important than you can imagine that you be on time you hear?"

Danny smiled. "Don't worry old timer, we'll be there."

He turned and skated off, leaving Terrance to worry about what he'd do if Danny wasn't there when it was time to go.

He pushed the thought from his head. *'He'll be there.'*

* * *

Terrance passed the laundromat on the way to his work spot, and as he walked past, saw the skeletal boxes with small squeaking wheels attached to them, the chariots for clothing. This triggered the thought in his head, *'Time to start gatherin'.*' He stayed his course, but his destination had changed. He decided it was time to make his way over to the Food 4 Less on Sixth Street for his first train car. He knew that that location in specific still ran a good deal of older carts, the ones without the locks that would freeze up if you tried to take em' past the invisible barrier around the parking lot. They were bigger than most other stores as well, and if Danny's little friend didn't show, they'd need all the room they could get.

He was passing his house when he saw Mad Dog stepping out from the bathroom up the hill.

"Mad Dog," he called out, "Wanna give me a hand?"

"Might as well," he replied with a smile, "ain't exactly too busy now am I?"

"Good," Terrance said. "Thinkin' we should hit the ole' Food 4 Less and grab ourselves a couple carts."

Mad Dog clapped his hands together, sending the sound reverberating throughout the underpass. "Let's do this."

Terrance stuck his message sign in his house, and they made their way down Alvarado about five blocks when the thought hit him.

"You know Mad Dog," Terrance said, throwing a glance at his friend. "I've known you for almost two years now, and I have never asked what your real name is."

Mad Dog stayed quiet for a moment, then in a shame laced whisper said, "Carroll."

"Carroll!?" Terrance replied in a blast.

"Yeah," Mad Dog replied, glancing around to see who had heard. "And don't you go fuckin' spreadin' it either."

They walked for another few minutes before the words screaming and clawing inside Terrance's throat finally tore themselves free. "Ain't that a girl's name?"

"Yeah mufukka, I know. My parents is Irish *aiight*. We got all kinds a fucked up names like Carey, and Kelly, and Frances. Fuckin unisexual names and shit dawg."

Terrance hadn't intended to get his friend riled up, and quickly apologized.

"Sorry brotha." He stopped walking and stuck out his hand. "Terrance."

Mad Dog stopped and gave him a shocked look. "Terrance? No wonder you go by T-Bone."

"Easy *Carroll*," he said leaning his head back.

"Fuck off," Mad Dog replied, puffing his chest out and letting a small grin escape through the street toughened façade, and then took Terrance's hand and shook it firmly. "Good to meet you officially T-Bone."

"Likewise Mad Dog," Terrance replied with a smile. "Now lets go build us a train."

Twenty minutes later they were walking up to the Food 4 Less parking lot. They'd taken carts a million times before, but there was something different about this time, something that made them feel as though they should move a little more carefully.

"So how you wanna do this?" Mad Dog asked as they entered the lot.

"Let's see if there's any in the corral behind that truck," he responded, nodding to the parked eighteen-wheeler just ahead of them.

They made their way around, and mixed in with a pile of carelessly discarded carts, were two without the plastic anti-theft attachments on their front wheels.

They shifted the carts around and fished out the two they needed, pushing them together.

"You go find another one," Terrance said. "I'll stay here and keep an eye out on these two, make sure they don't disappear."

"Word up," Mad Dog said, turning to make his way through the lot towards the other corral.

As he walked away the thought hit Terrance. *'Ya know, for being a skinny white dude with fiery orange hair and freckles, he talks more like a nigga than I do, and I'm black...'* Terrance chuckled to himself at the thought, following it up with, *'Man, talk about an identity crisis. Poor kid not only thinks he's black, but he's got a girl's name to boot.'* He almost let a laugh out when he saw Mad Dog coming back, pushing two carts in front of him.

He smiled and nodded in approvement, and when he walked up, said,

"Alright man, let's try and not get seen jackin' these carts if you know what I mean."

They pushed their stolen transports out of the lot, and back on to Alvarado. It took a little longer to get them back then it did to make their way there with the carts clacking up the sidewalk, not to mention that stretch of the road went up and over two large hills.

When they arrived back at the camp Terrance said, "Better hide these up the hill and cover em' with some brush. Don't want those Mexican guys in the flatbed comin' and collectin' up for cash."

Mad Dog agreed, and they carried the carts one by one up the side of the embankment, and broke down some branches on the large brush, covering the carts, and using fallen palm fronds to do the rest.

"Thanks Mad Dog," he said, slapping hands over a job well done. "I gotta get some work in before it gets dark, gotta save up all I can."

"I'm sure you could take Joe's spot, he's out runnin' around town, I don't think he'd mind."

"It's cool," Terrance said, "I got my regulars I can rely on, and I need all the cash I can make these next couple days."

He reached in his tent and grabbed his sign, and then made his way to his work spot where he spent the rest of the early afternoon spreading his message of the inevitable fate of mankind, which was responded to with laughing and pointing, and the occasion young hip kid snapping a picture of, undoubtedly to upload to their Instagram or Snapchat for a laugh. It didn't matter to Terrance however, just as long as more eyes were able to see his warning.

He called it quits, allotting himself enough time to make it to the surplus store before they closed. When he walked in the woman that had helped him before was behind the counter.

"You're back," she said with a quizzical look.

"Yep," Terrance said, shooting her a curt smile. "Another supply run."

He made his way to the back, and since he had more than enough water tablets, focused only on ready to eat meals, and a couple pairs of the expensive socks that would last years as long as he kept em clean.

He made his way to the front counter, and the woman gave him a strange look, asking, 'You wouldn't happen to know something we don't know?"

Terrance looked at her for a second, and then said, "Let's just put it this way Miss, when Friday rolls around, you might wanna make sure you're underground."

He picked his bag up off the counter and headed to the door. As he was walking out, he said, "Fallout shelter might be good," over his shoulder.

The bus ride back he kept thinking about Danny and Armando. He knew Danny would be coming, he just worried if he'd be there on time, and not held up waiting for his little girlfriend. Armando was the one that kept pulling at his strings. He knew there was nothing more he could say, but he feared spending the rest of his life knowing that there was a family that he knew, that he cared for, that died because he was another homeless guy with a crazy story that their father didn't listen to because he was jaded to the words of a bum.

He'd made it to his stop on Alvarado and stepped off the bus. He turned the corner to head towards his house when the ringing in his ear started up. Moments later he was standing in a seared wasteland, the street he was walking on now blackened and covered in pitch. There were cars parked neatly in rows, skeletons at their wheels, and in the intersection there was five or six cars all piled up together in a mangled heap of cauterized steel and deliquescent plastic.

He turned slowly around, shivering from an unseen cold.

Revelations

Where the bus he had previously just stepped off of was, was a macabre semblance, a contorted carcass full of the remnants of humanity caught unaware and helpless, posed like carbonized mannequins two by two.

Terrance shielded his eyes from the vapors of heat rising from the ground, spread as far as he could see, like concrete heated all day in the hot summer sun.

He put his hand over his face, and pressed his finger hard into his eye sockets, praying that the pain would release him from the abhorrent sight.

When he pulled his hands away, he was greeted by the color of normalcy, and the sounds of the crowded landscape came flooding back.

He walked in the direction of his house, his stomach again feeling like someone had filled it with warm yogurt left out too long. Every step he took he forced the vile, slushing concoction to stay its rest at the bottom of his twisting gut.

A few blocks down the road he stopped to sit on a small wall near the entrance to a motel. He felt dizzy, and the world around him spinning didn't help the liquid rollercoaster in his stomach. He hung his head between his knees and sat there, trying desperately to block everything out, everything except his plan for surviving.

After a short time his vertigo dissipated and he was able to make his way home. When he got there he crawled into his tent, pulled out his book and spent the next hour and a half reading before falling asleep.

Thursday the 27th

Terrance woke up. He had just been standing underneath an enormous statue of Jesus with his arms outstretched to his sides. He had stood under the symbol of protection as the world beneath him burned like the cities of Sodom and Gomorrah. He watched as the tiny islands that pockmarked the surface below ignited, and the fleshy earth covering them was seared away, leaving the molten remains below exposed. He watched as millions more were eradicated in a single breath from an angry star.

Now however, he was alone in his tent, covered in sweat, his sleeping bag puddled at his feet.

'This is our last day.'

Terrance got dressed and stepped out onto his patio. He walked two houses down and tapped on the front of Jimmy's tent.

"Jimmy," he called out, "you home?"

"Yeah homes," he answered, "Be out in second man."

Terrance waited.

A couple moments later the zipper to Jimmy's place dropped down and he came crawling out, his jail-etched tattoos showing beneath his wife beater.

"You get anything worked out?" Terrance asked.

Jimmy smiled, and opened the flap to his house. Just inside was a pile of orange vests, and four white L.A. County work helmets.

Terrance smiled.

"I kinda had to go back to my old ways for a minute," Jimmy said. "I ain't too proud of what I've done, but if this is important as you say it is, then fuck it, it won't matter tomorrow anyways."

Terrance looked at Jimmy, and with sincerity, said, "Thank you Jimmy. This helps a lot."

"Hey, de nada homes. You'd do the same for me."

He was right.

"Look," Terrance said, "When Mad Dog gets up, go with him to take care of the water situation. *Borrow* a dolly from the Home Depot, and get like four or five jugs of water. We're gonna need as much as you can get, and if you got any cash left, hit the 99 and get as much canned food as you can. Make sure whatever you get has a lot of protein in it ya hear?"

"Sure thing T-Bone," he replied.

"I gotta take care of some last minute things, but I'll be back here later. We need to load these carts up, and get em' over by the Hall of Records tonight, I wanna be ready to move in as soon as the sun comes up."

"Orelay," Jimmy responded, tilting his cleanly shaven head back, the tattoo of two hands together in a praying position showing itself for a split second as he did.

Terrance started making his way to the Tropical. He wore the unsettling burden of sadness like a heavy coat in the heat as he walked, feeling pity for every car that passed, and every house he saw. He knew what tomorrow would bring. He saw the unprejudiced gift of death and carnage that the sun was about to bestow on the planet. He knew that by late afternoon the next day, everything he had ever known would be gone, erased from history, blown away like the tuft of smoke from an extinguished match.

He made it to the corner and paused, deciding that this day was just as important as his birthday, and made his way to the tobacco shop on the corner. He bought a Swisher Sweet; the cognac flavored one, and asked if he could get four or five books of matches. The Brazilian guy working the counter was cool, and handed him a handful, much more than he had asked for. He said thank you and made his way outside. He had this feeling that he needed to enjoy everything that he loved one last time, because after tomorrow, he would never get the chance again; his only enjoyment would come in the form of memories that would soon fade to dust.

Revelations

He stepped up to the counter of the Burrito King and ordered a small horchata. As the guy at the counter was filling his cup he unwrapped his cigar, and struck a match. He lit the Swisher, and stared at the small tuft of flame for a moment. *'Funny. It's because of you that life on this planet is going to come to an end.'*

The man set his drink on the counter, and he passed two crumpled bills across, looking the guy squarely in the eyes and saying, "Thank you. Thank you for all the food and drinks you have made for me."

The guy looked at him puzzled and replied, "You're welcome."

Terrance then turned the corner of the building and started making his way to the Tropical. By the time he had gotten a few blocks down he had finished the rice drink, and dropped the cup into a bus stop garbage can. He continued on, savoring the residual taste, and the occasional wash of cognac flavored tobacco. A few minutes later he was at the café. As he walked up he saw

Armando working inside. He took another puff of the cigar, and then snubbed it out on the sidewalk, putting the rest of it in his pocket for later that evening, when the preparations had been finished. He walked into the café and made his way to the counter.

"Hey T-Bone," Armando said with a smile. "How's it goin' today man?"

Terrance walked up and stuck his hand out.

Armando looked slightly perplexed. He reached out and took Terrance's hand. "Uh, what's up man?" He asked, concern carried on his voice.

"My name's Terrance," he replied, grasping his friend's hand tightly. "There's few people that know that, I thought you should be one of em'."

"Uh, you're kinda scarin' me man," Armando said, not pulling his hand back. "Is this about our conversation the other day?"

Terrance smiled and let his hand drop, scoffing slightly as he did. "I just wanted to tell you, that you may not know it, but you've shown me more love than most others have, and I consider you one of my best friends." Tears started to well in his eyes as he spoke. "I lost my family fifteen years ago, because I made some stupid decisions, and let things get in the way of what was truly important, my wife and my son." He paused, his gaze falling to the floor for a moment. "I know that I'll never see them again, and you are so very lucky to have a family of your own. You protect them as best you can, you hear me? No matter what happens, you be there for them."

Armando stood at the counter, staring at his friend. Something inside him was welling up, and he felt the strings of tears behind his eyes being softly plucked. He nodded. "Um, hey man." He paused, reaching for a cup. "This one's on me." A tear worked its way to the surface. Gravity slowly pulled it downwards. He made his way around the counter and wrapped his arms around his friend, tears falling freely.

Donald Morrison

After a few moments he stepped back and nodded at his friend, wiping the salted moisture from his eyes, and making his way back around the counter.

Terrance stepped over to the airpot in silence, and pumped what would be his last cup of coffee into the cup, deciding not to add sugar or cream, so he could savor it for all of its flavor, then he turned to make his way outside, stopping while the door was open and turning to Armando. "Good bye Armando."

Armando nodded, whispering a faint good bye, and then Terrance hit the street.

He made his way back up Sunset to his work spot where he stood, mindlessly taking donations for the next few hours, trying to file the faces of those he saw in their commutes into his memory banks.

For the first time since he'd taken to spanging, he looked into the eyes of every person that looked at him. For three hours he wallowed in sadness, swimming though sorrow to collect the meaningless scraps

170

offered to him by the links that held this time numbered chain together.

When he looked at his watch it read 12:45. He left the intersection, knowing that he'd never spend another morning standing there, waiting for the light to turn red to collect change and dirty looks. As he walked back towards sunset his cardboard warning swung lightly on the signpost, swaying for all the fleeting world to read.

He sat silently on the bus, watching the landscape roll by, admiring the beauty of the cities architecture like he had never before. He watched the people getting on and off the bus, admired the casual conversations that started, and ended when one of the passengers had to exit at their stop. He watched as man and woman, child and adult, dark and light, tall and short, all made their way through the transport, all coexisting; yet not knowing each other. He reflected on the thought that he lived in a city with over six million people, yet most people only knew a handful of others.

When he arrived at his stop, he exited through the front, and thanked the driver for his trip, then made his way off the bus and into the store. The woman that had helped him wasn't there, and as he was making his way back to the MRE's, a man at the front called out, "Excuse me. Can I help you?"

Terrance turned around and responded, "No, thank you though," and then continued on to the back, where he grabbed another small case of dehydrated meals, and made his way back to the front.

He set the box on the counter, and the guy looked him up and down, and then said, "That's twenty-two fifty."

Terrance pulled out the cash and passed it across the counter, picked up the box and walked back out into the sun. He wanted to take another long stroll, but decided he had too much to take care of today, and besides, after tomorrow, there would be nothing left but strolling.

He sat at the bus stop waiting for the bus, and the thought crossed his mind for the first time. What if he was crazy? What if this whole time, he had come down with schizophrenia or something because of stress, or lack of proper nutrition? What if he was about to once again, ruin the lives of the people he cared about?

He sat mulling this over as the bus arrived, and then solemnly stepped inside.

He was riding in silence, when just before Sunset Junction, Danny came hopping aboard the bus. He had his headphones in and was tapping his fingers quickly to the music on his skateboard, and when he put his buss pass away and began his way to the back of the bus noticed Terrance. He pulled the music out of his ears and said, "T-Bone, what's up man? Where you headed?"

"Headin' back to the house," he replied, lifting the box of meals of the seat next to him so Danny could sit down.

"So we still on for tonight?" Danny asked.

Terrance nodded. "Yes sir."

"Awesome," Danny said, "My girl and I are looking forward to seein' what the tunnels are like. She's been Googling it all day."

"Googling?" Terrance asked.

"Eh, it's an internet thing."

"Oh," Terrance replied, not quite understanding. "Ok."

"So, I didn't exactly tell my girlfriend that we were going to the tunnels because you thought the world was going to end. Didn't exactly want to scare her you know, so I just told her that it's a good idea to always bring enough stuff for a couple weeks, just in case an emergency should happen and you get stuck. I told her it's like that with hiking and everything, so at least if this does happen, she'll have some extra clothes, and some girl stuff."

"That's good on you," Terrance said. "We're gonna start preppin' the carts soon as the sun goes down. Any word from your friend up the hill?

"Who? Donny?"

"Yeah, that's the one. The guy with the little red car."

"Yeah," Danny said slowly, "Don't think he's gonna make it; something about a party at his grandmas house. I didn't ask too much."

"That's fine," Terrance said. "We should have the carts prepped by eleven, and moving them downtown by midnight, so make sure your at my spot by no later than ten, you got that?"

"Ten it is," Danny replied. "Hey uh, look. This is where I'm getting off," he said, reaching up to pull the yellow cord, "I really hope you're wrong about this."

Terrance took a deep breath and looked at Danny. "So do I son, so do I."

He rode the rest of the way in silence, and got off at his usual stop, but instead of going home, he headed to the park for one last stroll. As he made his way around the lake, he looked at the people he had come to despise; the middle class transplants with their scattered tattoos, and colorful shorts with white boat shoes, the urban hippy moms with their eco friendly silver water bottles, the arrogant café workers cleaning up after the middle-class trash at the boat house. All of his contempt, and hatred had drained from him. All he felt now was pity and remorse. They had gone throughout their entire lives planning their futures, plotting the course that would lead them to old age and eventually death, but here they were, no more or less a person than him or anyone else they came in contact with. He thought about the pretentious waiter at the Brite Spot, and the inexcusably rude guy at the café at the Junction. He felt sorry for them. Their whole lives they felt they were above others, and yet tomorrow, none of that would matter, because once the flesh has burned, and the muscle and tendons are melted away, their bones will turn the same faded white, and bleach the same in the unprejudiced sun.

* * *

Revelations

Terrance sat on his bench for the better part of three hours, soaking in the sky's reflection across the water, and watching the birds frolic. He smiled as the occasional turtle would pop its head out of the surface, prefaced with tiny air bubbles that would mark its exit point. He watched as families strolled around the lake, and the health conscious couples would jog past, or pedal on their single speed bikes. He watched as people smiled, and held phone conversations, or read their book while walking. He sat and admired humanity for what it truly was, a beautifully complex arrangement of different personalities and personas.

When he realized he had to start preparing the train, he got up and slowly exited the park, taking one last look back, trying with all his power to capture the picture in his mind for all times sake.

Terrance made his way towards the camp, adding item after item to his mental clipboard.

His prominent concern was food. They would have enough water to get them by for quite some time, and enough tablets to last for at least a year; after that he was sure he'd be able to find more viable sources of fresh water. It was food however that concerned him the most. He knew the MRE's would only hold out so long, and that they would soon find themselves hungry. He had seen how the landscape looked after the blast, and knew that there would be no plant life left, and that it would be quite a while until it regrew, and had no idea how long the ash cloud would block the suns rays. He also knew that after watching the top layer of the oceans boil away, finding sustenance from the sea could prove to be equally challenging in the beginning, at least before the fish that had survived the sudden rise in temperature began to spawn again.

He walked down the street, his mind a smoke filled mess as he worked out different methods of survival. One thing he knew though, was if they could make their way to Australia, the could possibly find refuge, but how to do that when the harbor was going to end up a burned out skeleton was beyond him.

By the time he got back to camp it was close to six. The sun was beginning it's threatening descent, casting a thin layer of darkness through the sky, silently heralding the unannounced fury it was about to release the next time it showed its fiery glow.

As he walked up Mad Dog stepped out of his house with a half a roll of toilet paper in his hand. "Sup T-Bone? I got em," he said with an accomplished tone. Got six of dem bitches'."

"Nice." Terrance said. "Where they at?"

"Got em in my house, locked up safe and sound," he replied. "Told you that lazy mufukka be slippin'. This time, we just happened to be there."

Terrance nodded. "That's a good job Mad Dog, real good job."

"Hey, Mad Dog," Terrance said as he was turning around.

"Sup?"

"You seen Joe around?"

Mad Dog shook his head and shrugged. "Not since this mornin'. Said sumpin' bout havin' some shit ta' take care of." He paused. "And speakin' a which," he said, holding the paper roll up.

"Thanks man," Terrance replied, letting Mad Dog turn to make his way up the back hill towards the restroom spot.

He unzipped his front door and climbed inside. He began meticulously folding all his belongings, rolling them up so they'd fit inside his pack. He pulled the picture of his family from the ceiling and stared at it, falling back to a sitting position as he did. He stared at the photograph. It was taken on a Sunday trip to the nearby zoo. T.J. was standing next to a sign that read, Silverback Gorilla's, and the love of his life, Latisha was standing next to him with a big smile, her yellow Sunday dress tugged slightly to her right by the wind. T.J. had begged them to see the Gorillas; said he wanted to see them more than anything else in the world! He looked so happy in that picture.

Terrance stared at the photograph for a long while, and then wiped away the warm tears that had flowed their way down his face, and stuck the picture between the haunting story of the Torrance family, closed the book and tucked it into his bag, snug between his clean clothes. He gathered the rest of his things and packed them neatly into his bag, pausing to do one last check and then stepped back out onto his porch.

He had just finished zipping up his tent when Mad Dog came back down the hill and asked, "So when we gon' do dis?"

Terrance glanced at their houses, and then said, "We should probably pull the carts down around ten, have em loaded by eleven and start making our way downtown before midnight. I'm expecting a couple folks to meet us here. They're gonna be coming with us."

"You actually got people to believe you. Damn son. You *are* a silver tongued devil, ain't ya'?"

Terrance smiled. "Just a friend of mine and his little girlfriend. They're young, still in their teens, but I've known the boy for a few years now."

Mad Dog nodded. "That's whasup."

"Look," Terrance said, seriousness working its way behind his words, "if there's anything you feel you need to do, or anybody you gotta say goodbye to... I think now would be the time. You may still not believe me, but trust me, this is gonna be your last chance."

Mad Dog shrugged. "Nobody gave a fuck about me before, I don't give a fuck about them. They can burn in hell."

Terrance nodded. *'If you only knew...'*

"One of you fools wanna give me hand?"

Revelations

Terrance and Mad Dog turned to see Jimmy stepping out of a yellow taxicab. The shot each other a puzzled look and started towards their friend who was walking to the back of the car as the trunk popped open.

Terrance reached the back of the cab as Jimmy started setting paper bags on the sidewalk, unloading sack after sack from the trunk of the car.

"What's all this?" He asked, sticking his hands out to grab two bags from Jimmy.

"Call it supplies homie, just in case," Jimmy responded with a smile, pulling another two bags from the trunk.

Terrance handed them to Mad Dog and said, "Throw these in my place, I'll start bringing more. Let's wait till a little later to pull the carts down."

Mad Dog nodded, giving a single word reply. "Word." And then started towards the camp.

Jimmy pulled the last two heavy bags from the trunk and then closed it shut, walked to the front of the cab and tossed a handful of bills to the driver. "Enjoy it while you can homes," he said tapping the roof of the car signaling that he could leave. The cab driver then cut back into traffic, and disappeared.

Terrance picked up the last two bags and raised his eyebrows at Jimmy.

"Look homes," Jimmy said, "If shit's really gonna go down like you say it is, we gotta be ready. We can't be tryin to survive some end of the world shit and be runnin out of food homie." He paused, looking around to make sure nobody was in earshot. "I had to take care of business homie, but I got enough fedia to get us food for a month. We might not be eatin' steak and shit, but fuck it eh, it's better than nothing."

Terrance nodded, turned towards his house with the bags and said, "Thank you Jimmy, I was just freakin' out about food a little while ago. This is extremely good."

"Word Homie," Jimmy said, setting his bags down. "I still gotta go roll my shit up. When you wanna bounce eh?"

"In a couple hours man, just waiting on a couple more people," Terrance replied.

"For sure homes, in a minute then."

Terrance set the last two bags in his house. He knew that Jimmy had probably robbed someone to get the cash for all the food, but at this point, he knew it didn't matter much anyways, they weren't gonna get the chance to miss out on using it anyways. He was just happy to have enough food to lighten his worries a bit.

"Hey T-Bone."

Terrance turned to see Mad Dog following his voice towards the tent.

"What's up Mad Dog?" he replied, zipping his tent and standing up.

"I was just thinkin'. You said that everything's gonna be burned right?"

"Yeah," Terrance replied.

"So then that means that all the cows and shit'll be cooked right? So like, we can just cut strips off like jerky, and not have to worry as much about food?"

Terrance nodded. "Yeah, but the problem is it's gonna get so hot, that all the meats gonna be burned away. The only thing lefts gonna be the bones, but I like how you're thinkin', keep tryin' ta come up with ideas like that, might help keep us alive when this is over."

"Word," Mad Dog responded, turning to head back to his tent.

Terrance walked over to Jimmy's house and popped his head in. Jimmy was folding his three pairs of Dickies, stacking them neatly next to his wife beaters, white socks, and small stack of t-shirts he'd apparently picked up on his recent shopping spree.

"Yo Jimmy," He said, slightly startling his friend.

"Sup homie?"

"Look, I'm gonna take a walk real quick, I'll be back in an hour or so, if a younger kid and a girl show up, tell em I shot down the street and that I'll be back in a little while alright?"

"For sure homie," Jimmy replied, tilting his head back. What's the little homies name?"

"Danny," Terrance said. "Thanks Jimmy."

"No problem homie, I got you."

Terrance turned and made his way down Alvarado to MacArthur Park. He sat there at the edge of the water facing downtown and watched the twinkle of lights in the high-rise buildings. He thought about all the people that were working in them, and about the people that would be working the next day. He knew that they would be the first ones to go. They were the lucky ones. He watched the park residents making their illegal deals, and the Mexican guys on the corner trying to pitch their fake ID's. He watched the guys playing soccer under the white lights of the field across the street, and the bustle of people as they made their way in and out of the subway station. He admired how beautifully choreographed everything was, and wished that he had noticed it earlier, that he had had time to admire the beautifully organized chaos that was the human existence. He sat there for two hours, until his watch read 9:03, and then made his way to the McDonalds across the street from the park for what would be his last McDouble ever.

As he walked back to his house, he savored the flavor of the cheeseburgers he had so frivolously taken for granted all the years he had been homeless. He thought about all the people who had been able to survive simply because of the dollar menu at fast food restaurants, and how he had bitched and complained for years about having to eat this "crap". He thought about how blessed he was just to be alive to enjoy the food he was able to eat, and all those that had never gotten the chance; lost to wars or disease, or miscarried inside their mother's wombs.

He made it back to his house just shortly after 9:30, and called out to Jimmy and Mad Dog as he walked up. "Yo fellas, time to build our train."

They both came crawling out of Jimmy's tent. Mad Dog was complaining about how Jimmy cheated at cards, saying that next time he wasn't gonna take his eyes of him.

They met Terrance on the patio, and as they were about to turn around to grab he carts from the back hill, hey heard Joe call out from his house, "Movin' time?"

"Yeah," Terrance yelled, "Where the hell you been? I've was worried you'd gotten locked up or somethin'."

"Don't think I's gon' go tru da end a da world wit out getting' me some pussy do ya?" he said climbing out of his tent. "Shot me over to Bonnie Brae and got me some a dat cheap."

"You old dog," Mad Dog said with a laugh.

"This fool," Jimmy said shaking his head and tapping Terrance's arm.

"Money no good anymore right? Had my last fifteen," he said, once again flashing his large toothless grin.

Terrance exhaled sharply. "If I'd of thought about it, I probably would have done the same." He glanced at Jimmy who was still smiling as Joe staggered up smelling like vodka and moon pies. "Whatta ya say we build us a train?"

* * *

The group started loading all their belongings into the carts. Terrance loaded the food, organizing it so that it fit in the most functional way possible, and Mad Dog loaded two of the carts with the jugs of water. Jimmy was in charge of tying the carts together so they'd be easier to move, and while they all worked, Joe was in his house packing up last minute.

They finished loading the now constructed train, and then took the things they weren't going to take with them and set them near the stairs at the side of the overpass.

When everything was out of their houses; packed up or set aside, they broke them down and folded them up, putting them in the front cart that had two rope loops attached to the front for makeshift handles.

They finished up a little before ten and by this time Terrance was worried that Danny wasn't going to show up.

"He should have been here by now," he said to Jimmy who was doing a last minute check of the knots he had tied.

"Don't trip homie, he'll show. You know kids fool, they be late for their own funerals and shit."

Terrance nodded. "Lets give em' another hour. I did tell him we'd be leaving at latest midnight."

"How bout we just wait till they get here yeah?" Mad Dog replied.

"Thanks guys."

"It's all good homie, don't trip," Jimmy said with a head nod.

They sat there for the next hour and a half, talking about what they'd do if things really happened like Terrance said they were going to. They discussed heading south, trying to make it down past central America, through the Panama Canal to Brazil, and possibly crossing to Africa where it was less of a distance across the ocean; the only problem being that none of them had ever sailed before, so they would be relying upon luck to make it to their destination.

Mad Dog suggested trying basements of people's houses, bringing up the fact that some people prepped for natural disasters, and they might be able to find a stockpile of food that could last them a year or two until plants had time to grow again.

"We just gotta wait, we could start up a garden and shit, maybe catch some birds or somethin, keep em in cages, eventually they'll lay eggs and we can use em' for food."

"Yeah fool, you think we're really gonna find a house like that? That shit's only in the movies homie, this is real life. There ain't no secret basements with food and shit, and if there was, how the fuck you think we're gonna find it?" Jimmy said.

"Look dawg, I'm just tryin' to think of ideas *aiight*?"

Terrance jumped in, diffusing a very unneeded argument at an extremely inopportune time. "I think Mad Dog's actually got an idea. We can't check every house we go past, and to be honest, if it turns out like I've seen, there's not gonna be any houses to go through anyways cause they all gonna be burned down. But if we do come across any, I think we should check just to be sure. We never know."

"Well if we go through Mexico," Jimmy started, and we come across any of those big ass haciendas, we should definitely check em out. I know the cartels down there have big ass underground bunkers and shit eh. They build tunnels and shit to hide from the federales. We might find something there."

Terrance nodded. "That's a good idea Jimmy."

"Hey T-Bone, what time is it dawg?" Mad Dog asked.

Terrance looked at his watch. "11:40."

"Your little homeboy needs to show up soon pretty soon dawg."

"He'll be here," Terrance said, looking up the street to the distant sound of a skateboard making the distinct *clack* sound that came from someone doing a trick. As he looked up the block his heart lifted and the stack of weights pressing on his chest was lifted. Danny was coming his way riding slowly with a young Hispanic girl walking next to him.

"And speak of the devil," Terrance said.

A minute later Danny and his girlfriend came walking up.

"Hey T-Bone," Danny said. "This is my girlfriend Cindy."

"Nice to meet you Cindy," Terrance said, sticking his hand out.

She flashed a smile and shook his hand.

"And this is Jimmy," Terrance said, beginning the introductions.

"Sup eh?"

"and Mad Dog,"

"Sup."

"and this crazy old bastard is Guitar Joe."

Joe flashed his big grin and lifted his hand in a quick wave.

"You wanna throw your bags on the train?" Terrance asked, nodding to the carts all tied up and ready to go. "No sense truckin' em all the way downtown if'n you ain't got to."

"Sure," Danny said, setting his skateboard in the cart nearest to him and flipping his rather large pack off his shoulder and setting it in the cart before turning and helping his girlfriend with hers.

"So what route are we gonna take?" Danny asked after they had put their things on the train.

"Well," Terrance began, " I figure, we should at least get as close to downtown as possible without actually going into it. I think if we get to close, we stand a higher chance of getting stopped by the police, and we don't want that to happen, not tonight. I think we could probably stay at the park on Beaudry, which would put us about ten minutes away from the Hall of Records. We can get a few hours sleep at the park, and I'll set the alarm on my watch for seven o' clock, that way we can be there when they open at eight. Once we get there, we just have to figure out how we're supposed to get these carts inside, past security if here is any, and down into the tunnels without any problems."

"I have an idea," Danny said after a moment with a smile. "At eight o'clock, as soon as we see them open the doors, I'll call 911 and tell them there's a bag in front of the courthouse down the street, and that I think there's a bomb in it; that'll have every cop in the city that's on duty preoccupied. As soon as we hear the sirens, Cindy," he said, turning to her, "you're gonna run inside and tell the security guard that someone has been stabbed on the side of the building away from the entrance." He looked back to Terrance. "That way, security will be away from the front, and if he calls the police to report a stabbing before he goes to check, they'll be too busy looking for the bomb to bother with a stabbing." He paused, smiling as he spoke. "We'll be able to just push the carts right through the front door."

Terrance smiled and nodded. "You know what Danny," he said, pausing for a moment as his smile grew. "That idea just might be crazy enough to work."

"Damn dawg," Mad Dog said smiling and clapping his hands loudly together, "That's like some out of a movie type shit. For real dawg."

"And I can pretends I's stabbed real bad," Joe said, holding his stomach like he had just gotten stuck with a knife.

"No Joe," Terrance said, "You're gonna be with us, ain't nobody gotta pretend they were stabbed, we're just gonna tell the guard that so he leaves his post. You gotta be there to help us with the carts."

"Well," Joe said, still stuck on the idea of playing injured, "if you needs me ta act stabbed, I can do it."

"We know Joe," Terrance said smiling and patting him on the shoulder. "You just stay with us you hear."

Terrance looked at Danny and said, "I'm really glad you decided to come Danny." He paused momentarily, looking to Cindy. "And you too Cindy, real glad."

Danny nodded. He still didn't believe that the world was going to come to an end the next day, but as for an experience, and a story that he'd be able to tell for the rest of his life, he wasn't going to miss it.

Terrance looked at everyone that was standing with him. "So whatta ya say we get this train on the road?"

* * *

It was almost an hour before they made it to the park on Beaudry and Temple. The carts had made for their travel being three times slower than usual, and by the time they had made it, the train had been broken into two sections, one with the food and supplies, and the other with just the water and shelters.

They entered the park and headed for the baseball diamond. Then moved to an area where the bleachers stuck into the air, and pulled the carts underneath them, blocking their view from the street.

They group each found a place to rest near the train and unfolded the cardboard boxes they had brought with them and made makeshift beds for the next few hours. They sat and chatted for a short while, mostly asking Danny and Cindy a plethora of questions about where they were from, and what school they went to and things like that. It was almost two o'clock in the morning before they finally settled down for a few hours sleep, and when they dozed off,

Terrance dreamed again, this time he saw things from an outside view.

* * *

Terrance was floating in a vast expanse of silent black. It took a moment for his eyes to adjust to the ebony pitch, and it wasn't until the realized that the small pinpoints of twinkling white that he saw all around him were stars that he realized he was floating in space. He held out his invisible hands, and through the empty space saw the sun fading into focus, dim at first, then increasing in size until it was a blinding radiance.

He brought his non-existent hand up to shield his eyes from the heat and light when he saw what appeared to be a giant snake of molten fire begin piercing its way out from the surface of the sun, slithering across and connecting a quarter of the way across its face. It ebbed for a moment, slowly pulsing outwards before it swelled into a massive formless shape and erupted outwards, sending a giant burst of heat and energy flying into space directly towards him.

He prepared himself for the impact, wishing desperately for the hands and arms that should have been there to bring up in a futile attempt to shield himself from the coronal flare approaching him at over a million miles an hour. In an instant it was upon him. He felt the wave of eradicating heat blast through him, and he turned his vision to what lay behind him; it was the earth.

As he floated listlessly in space, his emotions welling up he watched the flare impact his home. It sent a wave of fire blasting over the globe, scorching away surface of the half that it hit, and bleeding back to the next quarter before being expelled around it.

In an instant he was on the other side of the planet, looking at the small area the devastation had been merciful to. He saw the continent of Australia and bottom half of Africa untouched by the superheated tide and realized these were the only places that were to survive what was almost an extinction level event.

He watched as a cloud formed within moments and began to blanket the earth. He watched in abhorrent horror, frozen in a liquid space as billions of lives were extinguished by a single, unforeseen, thermal blanket of fire.

He felt tears begin to form in eyes that weren't there, and an illusory mouth opening wide to release a silent scream into the dark void. He felt the cold breath of space beginning to envelope him as he drifted backwards into the dark.

Friday the 28th

When Terrance checked his watch it said 6:53. The sun had begun casting its rays through the sky and the morning commute was already at a mild roar.

Terrance sat there for a few minutes, letting his dream work its way into memory, and waiting for the beeping alarm of his watch to wake the others, and signal that it was time to start their mission.

He stood up and stretched, taking a heavy lungful of the morning air, and then his watch ignited with sound.

"Alright guys, time to move," he said, the reminiscent feeling of his time in the army peeking its head out for a moment.

Danny stretched as he opened his eyes, and then slightly shook his girlfriend awake, who yawned and wiped the sleep from hers. Mad Dog lay in bed scratching his crotch for a moment before quickly forcing himself to sit up, followed by Joe.

After a couple minutes Terrance walked over to where Jimmy lay, and tapped his foot against him, saying, "Jimmy! Time to get up man, gotta go."

He mumbled something and then rolled over onto his side, propping himself up with one arm and scratching his leg with the other.

"Damn homie, I just fell asleep," he said, slowly pulling himself to his feet.

Mad Dog chuckled. "We're gonna have to start calling you sleepy, dawg."

"Nah," Jimmy said, "Sleepy's my cousin homie."

"Gum?" Danny said digging a pack out of his bag. "Didn't think we'd have time to brush this morning, so I brought some."

Terrance and Jimmy declined, and Mad Dog looked over and asked, "What kind you got homie?"

"Tropical," Danny answered.

"That's wussup," Mad Dog replied, stepping forward with his hand out.

"Joe?" Danny asked, who replied by pulling his lips back as far as he could, exposing his two pink ridges with nothing between.

"Oh," Danny said, slipping the pack in his pocket and then bending down to pick up his pile of change and his cellphone.

"Everybody ready?" Terrance asked, receiving affirmative answers around. "Well then what we waiting for, lets do this.

Everybody grabbed their perspective carts and pushed them out of the field and back onto temple. Twenty minutes later they were parked across the street from their destination and were waiting for the guard to unlock the front door.

They sat there quietly, patiently waiting for the sentry to move from his post when a voice startled them.

"You guys got room for four more?"

Jimmy startled, spinning quickly, and Terrance turned his head to the sound of the familiar voice, his mouth opening slightly in surprise as he did.

"Armando!" he said, his eyes getting bigger. "Thank god."

He was walking towards them with a young woman and two children, both girls. Armando and the girl had large bags on their back and the two young girls each had small backpacks on. The youngest was carrying a small lunchbox.

He moved forward and embraced his friend, stepping back with a smile to ask, "And who do we have here?"

Armando stuck his hand in the direction of his family. "This is my wife Elena, and my daughters; Isabella and Zoe."

"Well it's very nice to meet you," Terrance said, receiving a smile from Elena, and a timid wave from the youngest. "My name's Terrance, and these are my friends, Mad Dog, Jimmy, Joe, Danny and his girlfriend Cindy.

Terrance was bewildered at the arrival of his friend and his family.

"So... What made you show?" he asked, curiosity tearing at him.

Armando let his gaze fall to the ground, and then brought it up to meet his.

Revelations

"I've known you for almost five years now, and of all the people I know, and friends that I have, you're probably the most level headed, honest, and down to earth one I have. So when you told me about your dreams, I couldn't quit thinking about if you were right. You've never lied to me, at least not that I know, you don't do drugs, and hell, most of the time you don't even wanna accept a free cup of coffee, so when you came in to the shop, and you said goodbye. There was something in your words that hit me. I knew you weren't lying, and you're right, I have to take care of my family however I can, and even if that means following a group of homeless guys into the basement of some building in downtown, well then..." He shrugged. "That's why we're here. People don't say goodbye like that to their friends unless they know something's *really* gonna happen, and they ain't gonna see em' again. You knew that was goodbye, and I could feel it, so I went home, told Elena that we had to pack up our things, and follow you to downtown, and that she'd just have to trust me on this one, so as much as I hope you're wrong about this, if you're not, just know that I'm gonna be sleeping on the couch for a while."

Terrance wanted to smile at his friends last words, but the seriousness of the situation pushed it back, and he responded by simply saying, "Thank you Armando."

"Of course T-Bone, like you said, I would do the same for you." He paused, glancing around. "So what's the plan?"

"T-Bone," Danny said, timing Armando's question perfectly, "Let's do this, our entrance is open."

Terrance looked at Armando and replied, "Looks like you're about to find out. Let's just hope this works."

Danny was already holding his phone to his ear as Terrance spoke, and when Armando heard his words his eyebrows came together and he shot Terrance a glance that showed how surprised, and lost he was.

Revelations

"Hello, operator? Yeah," Danny started, "Look, I'm in front of the courthouse on First and Hill. My friend just opened a backpack that we found in the bushes, and I think there's a bomb in it." He paused, giving the operator time to speak. "Yeah, I mean, it's a big bag, and there's some tubes that look like spray-paint cans with no labels, and a bunch of wires, and a red clock timer." Pause. "Yeah. Uh huh. No, trust me, when we opened it up we stepped back and then ran. No. No, the timer wasn't running, but you can tell it's a clock. It's one of those red LCD boards, like the kind inside a digital alarm clock." Pause. "No, we're far away now. Yeah. Ok... You got it. Thanks."

He brought the phone down from his ear, tapping the hang up button.

"Here we go," he said, throwing a glance at Cindy.

Less than two minutes later they heard the sirens.

"We give it two more minutes, at least until bomb squad shows up, then we move,"

Terrance said. He turned to Armando and said, "Would you like to put your bags in one of the carts? When we move we're gonna have to move quick."

Armando nodded, and turned to his wife, "Let me get your bag mama."

He took hers, and his daughters, and set them in the cart with two water jugs in it.

"You're good?" Terrance asked.

"Yeah," Armando replied, beginning to look a little nervous. "We're good."

It was three minutes later when the large black and white trucks with Los Angeles Police, Bomb Squad Division painted across their sides came pulling up down the street.

"We have about two minutes before the cops are up here blocking the street off," Terrance said. "We gotta move now."

"You got this babe?" Danny asked.

"Yeah," Cindy replied, running to the corner and then crossing over so it would look like she was coming from around the building.

Terrance and the rest waited on edge for the next minute to see what was gonna happen, when their worries were answered by the desk guard stepping out of the front doors and heading up the sidewalk to make his way around the building.

The front door opened a moment later, and Cindy popped out waving; signaling to them that it was clear.

"Go time," Terrance said, grabbing the cart in front of him and carefully rolling it off the curb, and pushing it quickly across the street, followed by the others.

Two minutes later they were all waiting by the elevators in the hallway just off the lobby. Terrance had sent Mad Dog, Jimmy and Joe down to the basement floor first, telling them to find the door to the tunnels when they got down there. They sat with nail biting tension as the elevators made their way back up, knowing that the security guard would be back at any moment, and that he was probably apt to be a little suspicious about the girl running in hysterically, and then getting out there to find absolutely nothing. Terrance's only hope was that the guard would see the commotion down the street, and hopefully stay outside to watch the show that was literally being put on for him.

Ding

Terrance pushed his cart into the elevator and had Armando and his family squeezed in. Just as the door closed the next car arrived. He climbed in, and hit B on the button pad, watching the lobby squeeze into a thin line as the door closed.

He silently worried on his way down that when he stepped out he'd see the group standing helplessly in the basement, blocked by a locked door, or even worse, one with an alarm on it.

As the car settled to the bottom and the door opened up he stepped out to see Jimmy holding a door at the end of the large hallway open, and only Armando and his family remaining to go through.

He rushed towards the entrance and gave Jimmy a look that said how glad he was to see the door open, and then made his way inside.

The tunnel was much larger than Terrance had imagined, almost big enough to drive a truck through. It was grey and smelled of old concrete. The group had stopped about a hundred feet in, and Terrance could see that from the angle he was approaching that the spaced out dim lights in the ceiling were heading at a downward angle. This was a good thing. He wanted as many feet between them and the surface as possible.

He approached and asked Joe, "Any idea where this bomb shelter is?"

"Well I aint's thinkin' there's a whole lot a options goin' on down here," he replied.

"Well let's keep goin'," Terrance said, grabbing the cart in front and pushing it down the massive corridor.

He heard the others chatting softly behind him, but his focus was entirely on finding the shelter. He passed two doors opposite each other that had bathroom signs on them and made a mental note of it, calling out, "Found the restrooms."

Ten minutes later they came to an intersection. Terrance paused, and then made a quick decision to take the one that continued going deeper into the earth.

They had made it about another twenty minutes in when they came across faded yellow and black sign on the wall that had the symbol for radiation, and black arrows pointing further down.

"It's this way," Terrance called out, a wave of relief flooding warmly into him.

They followed the hall until they reached a giant lead door at the end with the same sign, minus the arrows on it.

He approached and pulled hard on the lever. It gave an ancient groan and then slowly pulled backwards.

The room before them was massive, at least fifty feet across and a hundred feet back. There was some minor furniture, and old couch and come chairs that looked like they had been drug down by vagrants a long time ago, and stacks of green military style cots against the back wall. There was a small door on the right, which he assumed was another small bathroom, and boxes of who knows what piled near the entrance.

He pushed his cart inside and out of old habit called out, "Clear."

The rest followed him inside, each moving in and scouting the place as they did.

"Well lets start setting things up," Terrance said, pushing his cart to one side and making his way to the cots in the back. "We're gonna be here for a while,"

He pulled one for each of them out and brought them to the middle of the room and unfolded them.

Joe had already moved to one of the old office chairs against the wall and was pushing his feet off the floor, spinning slowly in circles. Armando had moved his family to the couch, and was pulling some type of game out of his bag for his daughters. Danny and Cindy were inspecting the bathroom.

"Alright everybody," Terrance called out, getting the rooms attention. "Get situated, and then lets sit down, eat a couple bars, and try and come up with a plan. Things are a little different now that we have the little ones with us, but we still need to think about what we're gonna do."

"Elena packed up some sandwiches," Armando said. "And we have a good amount of sweet tamales we brought for breakfast."

"That's sweet of you," Terrance said, his gaze falling to Elena. "Thank you."

"You're welcome T-Bone. It's the least I could do."

The group settled in, forming their own little spaces in the room, and when Terrance finally looked at his watch again, it said 9:20.

'*Not much longer...*' He thought quietly to himself.

* * *

The group had finished formulating a loose plan as to what to do if Terrance's visions actually happened, and had come to a mutual agreement that even with all the ideas in the world, they still wouldn't know what to do unless it happened. They had all settled into their own little routines, and Terrance made his way over to Danny and Cindy.

"How you guys holding up?" he asked.

"We're good," Danny replied. "Cindy can't wait to go check out the tunnels, but I told her we gotta wait a while till we can go do that."

Terrance nodded. "Your parents were ok with you being gone for the night?" he asked, delicately breaking the ice that had been shimmering between them.

"It's just my mom," she replied, pausing for a second. "She doesn't really care what I do."

"Oh," Terrance replied, caught off guard by her response.

"Yeah," Danny said, interjecting. "Her dad passed away a while back, and her moms kinda taken to pills and drinking."

"We never really got along anyways," Cindy said quickly. "I always got along with my dad more."

"Yeah," Terrance said. "It's funny how people tend to gravitate towards one of their parents more than the other. Probably has something to do with our genes or something, like maybe you had just a little more of your dad in you."

Cindy smiled. "Yeah, we were way more alike than my mom and I."

"What about your family T-Bone?" Danny asked. "I don't think I've ever heard you say what happened to them, and how did you end up being homeless?"

Terrance took a deep breath. He knew he was in for a long conversation, but down here in the stomach of the earth, all they had was time, and waiting, so he began.

"You know how I don't drink much, and I don't do drugs Danny?" he began.

"Yeah," Danny responded.

"Well, bout fifteen years ago, I used to have a pretty bad drinkin' problem, and was doing my fair share of marijuana smoking and cocaine." He paused, reflection flashing through his eyes. "Well, the person I was closest to, other than my wife and son of course was my brother, Jerome. You see, we were really close, talked every day, went fishing all the time, you name it, we were typical brothers." He paused again, sadness welling up behind his words. "One day I get a phone call that he'd been hit by a car over in Charlotte. He was crossing the street to get us some new equipment for a trip we'd been planning, and had been hit by some lady talking on her cell phone, not paying attention to where she was going. He was dead before the ambulance even arrived."

Danny sat quietly, and Cindy tapped his leg, whispering that she was going to go to the restroom. He nodded quickly and then turned his attention back to Terrance.

"Needless to say, that put me in a real bad way," he continued. "I went off the deep end; found myself on a two week bender. Musta drank my bodyweight in rum. Well, before that I'd been managing a mattress store in Raleigh, was doin' pretty good for myself to, making forty a year, full benefits for my family and I. See, I was the smart one in my family. I went to college, busted my butt to get good grades, and graduated from UNC with a degree in business finance." He paused again. "My brother dyin', that just put a wrench in everything. So one night, I'm at the store late. I'd closed up shop, and was having drinks with this younger girl that worked for me; hell, I can't even remember her name now, but anyways, I guess I drank myself into a blackout, and when I woke up, My wife Latisha was standing at the foot of one of the stores display beds, and I was lyin' there buck naked next to that girl." He paused, shaking his head as he scoffed softly to himself.

"Damn," Danny said.

"Damn's right," Terrance replied.

"Turns out I hadn't locked the door, and the bed we was layin' on, was in the middle of the showroom, so everyone that walked past that morning saw my naked ass curled up next to some young white girl and an empty bottle of Captain Morgan. One of Tisha's friends had been the one to deliver the news via telephone."

"Whew..." Danny said, shaking his head slowly as he brought his hand up to rub the back of his neck. "Damn..."

"Yeah. Needless to say, I didn't have a home to go to after that." He took a deep breath, exhaling slowly. "Next day she filed for divorce, and took custody of T.J.; Terrance Junior was his name, and had all my stuff sent to a lock up facility at the edge of town. There was nothing I could do. I couldn't stay there, no one was gonna hire me after what I'd done, and even though it wasn't a tiny community, word still spread pretty fast about the mattress store guy that got caught cheatin' by his wife in the middle of the store at eight in the mornin'. I just grabbed what I needed, and made my way out here to L.A. I tried finding work for a while, held a couple lousy jobs, and then found myself in a bottle again. Next thing I knew, I was living on the street, making about thirteen an hour spanging, and not having to worry about rent, or bills, or my past creeping up on me, so I just decided to stay with it. And here we are now."

Danny stayed quiet for a minute. "Have you ever tried contacting your wife again, trying to fix it?"

"No," Terrance said defeated. "What would I say? Hey sweetheart, I've been homeless, living on the streets in California for the last fifteen years, I was wonderin' if I could come home now?" He smiled. "No, that was another life, this is who I am now."

"Don't you miss your son?" Danny asked.

"I used to, but it's been so long, he probably doesn't even know anything about me. He was two when I left. I'd just be another stranger to him, one that just happened to have his name."

"Wow," Danny said, feeling almost sorry for asking. "I'm sorry T-Bone."

"Yeah, well, you know what they say. Once you hit rock bottom, stones don't float, so most of the time, you just end up stuck there. But you know, it ain't so bad. I got my buddy's that I look out for, and friends like you that remind me how the world could have been for me. I mean, you're about my son's age. What are you, sixteen, seventeen?"

"Seventeen," Danny replied.

"See, you're exactly the same age my son would be now." He paused, taking another breath, realizing it was getting warmer. "Everything happens for a reason."

All of the sudden the lights went out, and Terrance could feel the sweat beginning to bead across his forehead.

"Somebody grab on of them candles," he shouted.

"Danny!?" Cindy yelled from across the dark room.

"I'm right here babe, just stay there and wait for us to find some light."

There was a flicking sound as someone brought a lighter to life, and when Terrance looked over, he saw Mad Dog holding the delicate flame and moving towards one of the carts.

It was getting hotter, and Terrance realize the air was getting so warm his throat was beginning to tingle with every breath.

"Quick," he called out, "breath through your shirt."

He heard Armando telling his daughters that it would be ok, they just had to breath like *"this"*, as he folded his shirt up and brought it to his face, covering his nose and mouth.

A few moments later the glow in the room got brighter as Mad Dog lit two more of the candles he had pulled from the bag.

Cindy rushed to Danny, and everyone stayed still, huddled in place. There was a hush in the room as everyone tried to form a rational explanation of what had just happened, suddenly realizing that Terrace had been right. The world above was on fire...

The group sat silently, hoping that the temperature didn't continue to rise, and that when they made their way back up, that it wouldn't be as bad as Terrance had described.

The temperature in the room continued to rise. Terrance sat on the floor, slowly rocking back and forth as he worried that they might not have gotten deep enough. Then after a few minutes, the heat plateaued, leaving the inside of the cement walled shelter feeling like a steam room that had been heated without water being poured over the lava stones.

For the next hour they all sat in silence, the candles casting their shadows eerily across the room, giving movement to the blank walls.

Terrance looked around the room. Danny was holding his girlfriend, Armando was kneeling in front of his family on the couch, their heads hung in prayer and Jimmy was sitting on his cot with his legs tucked underneath him across from Joe who was sleeping.

Part of Terrance wanted to go up to the surface to check and see how bad the damage was, but he realized, in every one of his visions he had only seen the fire beginning, and had no idea how long the blast had lasted, so he decided it better to wait until the temperature in the shelter returned to normal, signaling that the air outside had cooled back down to a safe level. Instead he moved to the cart that had his backpack in it, fished it out, opened it up and dug out his book; sinking back into the snow covered Overlook while the world around him flittered in the candlelight's shadows.

'Fitting,' he thought. *'I'm reading a story about the complete breakdown of a family secluded from the rest of the world, and here I am, amidst the complete breakdown of society, and destruction of the world, while forming a new family of my own.*

He took a deep breath and pulled the photograph page marker out without looking at it, afraid that it might cause him to break down into tears, and knowing that it was now more than ever that those around him needed him to remain strong. He couldn't afford for those that he brought down here to lose hope because their leader had begun to fall apart.

He set the photograph face down on the cot next to him and instantly transported himself back to the mountains of Colorado, and the fraying sanity of the Torrance family.

* * *

227

Terrance didn't realize he had fallen asleep till he looked around himself, and saw that he was standing in a foreign wasteland. The landscape was burnt, but not a fresh smoldering kind, more like the kind you see when you stumble across a campsite that hadn't been used in a long time, but still had the burnt remains of a campfire laying in the pit.

He looked around for a moment, puzzled by the change in scenery, and then the sky that caught his eye. In every vision he had, the sky turned a dark grey, eclipsing the suns light, and turning the landscape almost instantly into a metropolitan nightfall, not quite pitch black, but like a summers evening in a city full of lights. This time however, in this vision, the sky had returned to its azure hue, spotted with white cotton tufts. It was clear, and untouched by the acrid smoke that had filled his visions prior.

He took a few steps, crunching through the scorched kindling when a color other than grey or black caught his eye; it was green.

Just ahead of him, about four paces was a small strand of green. It was sticking out of a bare spot on the ground about an inch into the air.

Terrance held his breath as he approached the small sprout and kneeled down to get a closer look, the feeling of excitement and hope welling up inside him.

He stared at the new growth for a moment before standing up quickly and looking around for the rest of his group.

As his eyes looked behind him he saw a small hill, and somehow knew that his friends, his new family were just over it. He could feel their presence, and didn't know how, but new they were just a little ways away, and that news of his finding was about to change everything. He smiled, and began his slow trek towards the hill as the sounds of the shelter slowly invaded his dream, pulling him softly back to the dark room he was in.

"T-Bone," he heard coming from the cot across from his. "Hey T-Bone."

He shook the sleep out and sat up slowly. "What's up Jimmy?" he asked.

"Sorry to wake you homes, but the group was just wonderin' when we were gonna go up and check."

Terrance stretched and brought his hands to his face, rubbing it deeply, and then let his watch fall into view. It read 4:45 P.M. He had slept longer than it felt.

He took a deep breath and looked around the room. At this point everyone had gotten accompanied with each other, and Cindy was sitting with Elena and the kids chatting away, and Danny was sitting with Armando sharing a tall can of Bud Light that he had apparently brought along. Mad Dog and Joe were playing rummy on a cot they had pulled between them to make a table, and he could see the cards on the cot where Jimmy had been sitting before he got up to wake him from his slumber.

Terrance was happy that everyone seemed to be getting along. He had been worried at first, thinking that Danny's girlfriend and Armando's family would be a little put off by the rag tag group of homeless guys they would be sharing a small space with for the next day. It was a relief to see that wasn't so. He supposed that, to truly kind people, situation and appearance didn't dictate a person's value as a human. He had put together a good group.

He slowly stood, taking a deep breath and realizing that the air had cooled down a bit. He was still afraid to make his way back up to the surface; fearful to see the world he had already experienced in his visions. He was afraid for the others who had no idea what they would soon witness.

He cleared his throat, unintentionally gathering the attention of the others. The heat had dried his throat, and when he woke it felt like he had a fine layer of dust residing down his windpipe.

As he walked towards the cart with his bag he realized all eyes were upon him.

He held his index finger in the air, signaling that he would speak in a moment, and fished out a bottle of water from his pack, taking two large gulps, following them up with a relieved sigh as the warm liquid worked its way down the arid tube he was attempting to swallow through.

He looked into the eyes of every member individually before beginning his words.

"So I can only assume by the heat wave we felt, that everything I've been having visions of has happened. I had prayed that it wouldn't, but I can only assume that the world above is now gone."

Cindy grabbed Danny's arm and Terrance heard her ask him, "What's he talking about? What does he mean the world's gone?"

He continued. "For the first time in my life I had hoped that I was just going crazy, that my time on the streets had finally taken its toll on this old mind, but I'm afraid that ain't so." He paused, glancing between the group again. "I can't prepare you for what I've seen, and for the rest of my life, however long that may be, I have to live with the fact that you all are the only ones I could save." Sadness entered his face. "I tried. God I tried... But no one would listen to me." He paused, taking a deep breath and looking to his feet. "I guess in the end, it was my insignificance in the world that doomed them to their fate." He looked up to the eyes staring back at him. "But I'm blessed to have been able to save those that of you that were closest to me; all of you."

"There's still a chance you could be wrong T-Bone. For all we know, it was just a really strong heat wave, and when we get back up there, it'll be nothing more than really bad sunburns and some power outages for a while."

"I hope so Armando, I really do." Terrance replied, his eyes pleading with Armando's to be wrong about everything. I think we should give it another hour or so before we head back up, but I think just in case, for now, we should leave our supplies down here." His following words came out sounding fake and hollow to him. "Just in case the security guard's still up there, that way we don't come walking out of the stairwell with a bunch of stuff, giving him an excuse to call the police on us. This will give you guys a chance to walk out of here like nothing happened." He looked at Danny and Cindy, and Armando and his family as he said it.

They all agreed, and settled back into the conversations and card games they had been enjoying.

Terrance walked over and carefully placed his hand on the thick lead door, checking for outside heat. It was still warm.

He turned and made his way back over to his cot and sat down. He thought about setting his alarm, but didn't want to start his journey upwards on a startled note, so he just decided to check the time every now and then. He sat there and tried to clear his mind, mentally preparing himself in the same manner he had been becoming accustomed to before lying down to sleep at night. He knew what was coming; he was just hoping to postpone it for as long as possible.

* * *

Terrance stood up and made his way to the entrance, eyes locked in conversation breaking their gaze to follow him to the door.

He placed his hand against the cool lead and held it there for a moment, taking a deep breath and turning to the group that was now watching him intently.

"It's time," he said, almost reluctantly.

The group slowly gathered itself to its feet, Armando and his family strapping their bags back on, and Danny doing the same with Cindy.

Terrance didn't bother putting his bag on; he knew he would be coming back down for his stuff soon.

He heard Danny tell his girlfriend that it'd be ok, that it was just a heat wave and not to worry. He knew just how wrong he was. It *wasn't* gonna be ok. The earth above was black now, an ashen, scorched out reminisce of its former self, void of life, and barren of breath.

Terrance slowly pushed the lead barrier open; a high pitch squeak of unused hinges echoing loudly into the silent passage.

He stepped out, and led his group down the hallway that just earlier that morning had been filled with the energy of adventure and mystery, buzzing with the residual excitement of their covert operation.

They made their way down the large corridor, pausing at the intersection, and then making their way to the elevator that had brought them below.

When they arrived Danny reached out and instinctively hit the button as Terrance scanned the doors to see which one said stairwell.

"Nothing," Danny said, "No power."

"Stairs are this way," Terrance said, pushing a door open a few feet away.

Jimmy stepped forward with the flashlight he had fished out of his bag. "Let me take a look."

He stepped into the stairwell and flashed the light up as far as he could see, and then said, "Looks clear," before stepping in and making his way slowly up the stairs.

Mad Dog followed the group up in the rear with a large glass encased candle with a picture of the Lady of Guadalupe wrapped around it. He was the first to break the silence of the ascent.

"Smells like smoke," he said, his words bouncing off the metal stairs and railing.

Jimmy reached the top and waited for Terrance. When he got to the door that lead into the Hall of Records main lobby he reached his hand out and held it flat against it, feeling for heat. It was cool to the touch.

He took a deep breath and slowly twisted the knob, pushing the door inwards.

As the portal opened up, his eyes fell on a scene much more intense that any of his visions had experienced in the past week.

Jimmy looked past him, and he heard him whisper something in Spanish.

He fought for words, but the distorted reality sprawling in front of him stole them away before his mind had time to bring them forth to his vocal chords.

The building he entered into still stood, the thick concrete and steel structure unphased by the blast of heat, but everything inside of it had been incinerated; an, ashen mirage of its former self.

He stepped in dazed, as the reality of the situation began to set in. He walked through the burnt out building not looking back as he heard the gasps coming from the girls behind, or as Armando's girls began to cry. He walked silently, pulled towards the entrance to the building by an invisible tether, the blackened world unfolding before him.

Ash was falling like a light snow as they made their way past the space that had been occupied by the security officer and was swirling through the air, sticking lightly to their clothing. There was an uneasy quiet in the air, a contrast blaring against the usual noise coming from the chaotic downtown in the early afternoon. The only sound was coming from their footsteps as they clicked across the marble tile, slowly making their way towards the street out front, and the world that waited for them.

"My god," Terrance heard Armando say, just below a whisper behind him as he stepped out onto the sidewalk that lined what was just a few hours ago, a busy Hill Street. Now it was desolate; empty and still, save for the flakes of ash falling softly, lightly covering the landscape below.

Terrance looked down the street to where the bomb squad had previously been, and saw the vehicles still parked in place, only now they shared the same ebony tint, with a boiled, rust colored brown across the tops where the paint had boiled away.

Scattered along the scene were the remains of what were the officers that had been called out. Terrance could tell by the glint of what he realized were badges and guns reflecting in the dim light.

The city was dark, and there were no windows left in any of the buildings, just empty shapes, standing like oversized scaffoldings next to each other.

Terrance dug in his pack and pulled out a scarf, wrapping it around his face to filter out the ash, and turned to the others who began to do the same.

"You were right..." Danny whispered, as he stepped next to him while wrapping a t-shirt around his mouth and nose.

Terrance stayed quiet for a moment, and he spoke softly, his words carrying on the quiet breeze to the others. "We stay here until the rain stops, then we head south."

Danny looked at him puzzled and asked, "What rain?" and then he heard the thunder.

Donald Morrison

Epilogue

Six months had passed since the initial blast nearly wiped civilization from existence. The group of survivors stood at the entrance of the Recife Port, in Recife Antigo Brazil. They had walked over four thousand miles, and had lost two of their members, Guitar Joe, who died in his sleep shortly after beginning the journey, and Armando's youngest daughter to a fever while crossing through El Salvador.

They had managed to find provisions along the way with Jimmy's advice of searching the large haciendas, and managed to build a small stockpile of canned goods, enough to last them another few months.

They had built carts from pieces of old bicycles and handcarts they found while leaving Los Angeles, and managed to keep them in working order, using parts they found along the way to repair them.

They had made it as far as San Diego before the rain began to burn their skin; the carbon filled smoke blocking out the sky,

242

turning the falling droplets into an acidic wash.

The group had to take shelter for almost a month in the burned out Naval base just outside the city while the sky dropped its corrosive liquid across the landscape. The rain eating away much of what the fire had missed.

They now had three new members in the group; a man named Rodrigo, and his wife and son that had survived the blast because they had just happened to be taking a cave tour at Lanquín Cave in Guatemala when it happened, and crossed paths with Terrance and the others as they were heading south.

Now however, they stood at the remains of an old port, staring at the sunken husks of giant cargo ships, and burned out skeletons of skiffs and fishing boats lining the shore.

Terrance let his head drop down and whispered the words, "Will this ever end?" to himself. As he stared at the ground between his feet, he thought about the single blade of grass he had seen in his last vision.

He turned to the others and said, "This is where we sail."

ALSO BY DONALD MORRISON:

RABID LANDS

THE JOURNAL

GREY ZONE

OUROBOROS

JOURNEY THROUGH THORNS

DAWN OF THE MAGI